FRENCH ART

W.C. BROWNELL

Contents

FRENCH ART

BY

W.C. BROWNELL

I

CLASSIC PAINTING

I

More than that of any other modern people French art is a national expression. It epitomizes very definitely the national aesthetic judgment and feeling, and if its manifestations are even more varied than are elsewhere to be met with, they share a certain character that is very salient. Of almost any French picture or statue of any modern epoch one's first thought is that it is French. The national quite overshadows the personal quality. In the field of the fine arts, as in nearly every other in which the French genius shows itself, the results are evident of an intellectual co-operation which insures the development of a common standard and tends to subordinate idiosyncrasy. The fine arts, as well as every other department of mental activity, reveal the effect of that social instinct which is so much more powerful in France than it is anywhere else, or has ever been elsewhere, except possibly in the case of the Athenian republic. Add to this influence that of the intellectual as distinguished from the sensuous instinct, and one has, I think, the key to this salient characteristic of French art which strikes one so sharply and always as so plainly French. As one walks through the French rooms at the Louvre, through the galleries of the Luxembourg, through the unending rooms of the *Salon* he is impressed by the splendid competence everywhere displayed, the high standard of culture universally attested, by the overwhelming evidence that France stands at the head of the modern world aesthetically--but not less, I think, does one feel the absence of imagination, opportunity, of spirituality, of poetry in a word. The French themselves feel something of this. At the great Exposition of 1889 no pictures were so much admired by them as the English, in which appeared, even to an excessive degree, just the qualities in which French art is lacking, and which less than those of any other school showed traces of the now all but universal influence of French art. The most distinct and durable impression left by any exhibition of French pictures is that the French aesthetic genius is at once admirably artistic and extremely little poetic.

It is a corollary of the predominance of the intellectual over the sensuous instinct that the true should be preferred to the beautiful, and some French critics are so far from denying this preference of French art that they express pride in it, and, indeed, defend it in a way that makes one feel slightly amateurish and fanciful in thinking of beauty apart from truth. A walk through the Louvre, however, suffices to restore one's confidence in his own convictions. The French rooms, at least until modern periods are reached, are a demonstration that in the sphere of aesthetics science does not produce the greatest artists--that something other than intelligent interest and technical accomplishment are requisite to that end, and that system is fatal to spontaneity. M. Eugene Veron is the mouthpiece of his countrymen in asserting absolute beauty to be an abstraction, but the practice of the mass of French painters is, by comparison with that of the great Italians and Dutchmen, eloquent of the lack of poetry that results from a scepticism of abstractions. The French classic painters--and the classic-spirit, in spite of every force that the modern world brings to its destruction, persists wonderfully in France--show little absorption, little delight in their subject. Contrasted with the great names in painting they are eclectic and traditional, too purely expert. They are too cultivated to invent. Selection has taken the place of discovery in their inspiration. They are addicted to the rational and the regulated. Their substance is never sentimental and incommunicable. Their works have a distinctly professional air. They distrust what cannot be expressed; what can only be suggested does not seem to them worth the trouble of trying to conceive. Beside the world of mystery and the wealth of emotion forming an imaginative penumbra around such a design as Raphael's Vision of Ezekiel, for instance, Poussin's treatment of essentially the same subject is a diagram.

On the other hand, qualities intimately associated with these defects are quite as noticeable in the old French rooms of the Louvre. Clearness, compactness, measure, and balance are evident in nearly every canvas. Everywhere is the air of re-serve, of intellectual good-breeding, of avoidance of extravagance. That French painting is at the head of contemporary painting, as far and away incontestably it is, is due to the fact that it alone has kept alive the traditions of art which, elsewhere than in France, have given place to other and more material ideals. From the first its practitioners have been artists rather than poets, have possessed, that is to say, the constructive rather than the creative, the organizing rather than the imaginative temperament, but they have rarely been perfunctory and never common. French painting in its preference of truth to beauty, of intelligence to the beatific vision, of form to color, in a word, has nevertheless, and perhaps *a fortiori*, always been the expression of ideas. These ideas almost invariably have been expressed in rigor-ous form--form which at times fringes the lifelessness of symbolism. But even less frequently, I think, than other peoples have the French exhibited in their painting that contentment with painting in itself that is the dry rot of art. With all their ad-diction to truth and form they have followed this ideal so systematically that they have never suffered it to become mechanical, merely *formal*--as is so often the case elsewhere (in England and among ourselves, everyone will have remarked) in instances where form has been mainly considered and where sentiment happens to be lacking. Even when care for form is so excessive as to imply an absence of character, the form itself is apt to be so distinguished as itself to supply the element of character, and character consequently particularly refined and immaterial. And one quality is always present: elegance is always evidently aimed at and measurably achieved. Native or foreign, real or factitious as the inspiration of French classicism may be, the sense of style and of that perfection of style which we know as elegance is invariably noticeable in its productions. So that, we may say, from Poussin to Pu-vis de Chavannes, from Clouet to Meissonier, *taste*--a refined and cultivated sense of what is sound, estimable, competent, reserved, satisfactory, up to the mark, and above all, elegant and distinguished--has been at once the arbiter and the stimulus of excellence in French painting. It is this which has made the France of the past three centuries, and especially the France of to-day--as we get farther and farther away from the great art epochs--both in amount and general excellence of artistic activity, comparable only with the Italy of the Renaissance and the Greece of an-tiquity.

Moreover, it is an error to assume, because form in French painting appeals to us more strikingly than substance, that French painting is lacking in substance. In its perfection form appeals to every appreciation; it is in art, one may say, the one universal language. But just in proportion as form in a work of art approaches perfection, or universality, just in that proportion does the substance which it clothes, which it expresses, seem unimportant to those to whom this substance is foreign. Some critics have even fancied, for example, that Greek architecture and sculpture--the only Greek art we know anything about--were chiefly concerned with form, and that the ideas behind their perfection of form were very simple and elementary ideas, not at all comparable in complexity and elaborateness with those that confuse and distinguish the modern world. When one comes to French art it is still more difficult for us to realize that the ideas underlying its expression are ideas of import, validity, and attachment. The truth is largely that French ideas are not our ideas; not that the French who--except possibly the ancient Greeks and the modern Germans--of all peoples in the world are, as one may say, addicted to ideas, are lacking in them. Technical excellence is simply the inseparable accompaniment, the outward expression of the kind of aesthetic ideas the French are enamoured of. Their substance is not our substance, but while it is perfectly legitimate for us to criticise their substance it is idle to maintain that they are lacking in substance. If we call a painting by Poussin pure style, a composition of David merely the perfection of convention, one of M. Rochegrosse's dramatic canvasses the rhetoric of technic and that only, we miss something. We miss the idea, the substance, behind these varying expressions. These are not the less real for being foreign to us. They are less spiritual and more material, less poetic and spontaneous, more schooled and traditional than we like to see associated with such adequacy of expression, but they are not for that reason more mechanical. They are ideas and substance that lend themselves to technical expression a thousand times more readily than do ours. They are, in fact, exquisitely adapted to technical expression.

The substance and ideas which we desire fully expressed in color, form, or words are, indeed, very exactly in proportion to our esteem of them, inexpressible. We like hints of the unutterable, suggestions of significance that is mysterious and import that is incalculable. The light that "never was on sea or land" is the illumination we seek. The "Heaven," not the atmosphere that "lies about us" in our mature age as "in our infancy," is what appeals most strongly to our subordination of the intellect and the senses to the imagination and the soul. Nothing with us very deeply impresses the mind if it does not arouse the emotions. Naturally, thus, we are predisposed insensibly to infer from French articulateness the absence of substance, to assume from the triumphant facility and felicity of French expression a certain insignificance of what is expressed. Inferences and assumptions based on temperament, however, almost invariably have the vice of superficiality, and it takes no very prolonged study of French art for candor and intelligence to perceive that if its substance is weak on the sentimental, the emotional, the poetic, the spiritual side, it is exceptionally strong in rhetorical, artistic, cultivated, aesthetically elevated ideas, as well as in that technical excellence which alone, owing to our own inexpertness, first strikes and longest impresses us.

When we have no ideas to express, in a word, we rarely save our emptiness by any appearance of clever expression. When a Frenchman expresses ideas for which we do not care, with which we are temperamentally out of sympathy, we assume that his expression is equally empty. Matthew Arnold cites a passage from Mr. Palgrave, and comments significantly on it, in this sense. "The style," exclaims Mr. Palgrave, "which has filled London with the dead monotony of Gower or Harley Streets, or the pale commonplace of Belgravia, Tyburnia, and Kensington; which has pierced Paris and Madrid with the feeble frivolities of the Rue Rivoli and the Strada de Toledo." Upon which Arnold observes that "the architecture of the Rue Rivoli expresses show, splendor, pleasure, unworthy things, perhaps, to express alone and for their own sakes, but it expresses them; whereas, the architecture of Gower Street and Belgravia merely expresses the impotence of the architect to express anything."

And in characterizing the turn for poetry in French painting as comparatively inferior, it will be understood at once, I hope, that I am comparing it with the imaginativeness of the great Italians and Dutchmen, and with Rubens and Holbein and Turner, and not asserting the supremacy in elevated sentiment over Claude and Corot, Chardin, and Cazin, of the Royal Academy, or the New York Society of American Artists. And so far as an absolute rather than a comparative standard may be applied in matters so much too vast for any hope of adequate treatment according to either method, we ought never to forget that in criticising French painting, as well as other things French, we are measuring it by an ideal that now and then we may appreciate better than Frenchmen, but rarely illustrate as well.

II

Furthermore, the qualities and defects of French painting--the predominance in it of national over individual force and distinction, its turn for style, the kind of ideas that inspire its substance, its classic spirit in fine--are explained hardly less by its historic origin than by the character of the French genius itself. French painting really began in connoisseurship, one may say. It arose in appreciation, that faculty in which the French have always been, and still are, unrivalled. Its syntheses were based on elements already in combination. It originated nothing. It was eclectic at the outset. Compared with the slow and suave evolution of Italian art, in whose earliest dawn its borrowed Byzantine painting served as a stimulus and suggestion to original views of natural material rather than as a model for imitation and modification, the painting that sprang into existence, Minerva-like, in full armor, at Fontainebleau under Francis I, was of the essence of artificiality. The court of France was far more splendid than, and equally enlightened with, that of Florence. The monarch felt his title to Maecenasship as justified as that of the Medici. He created, accordingly, French painting out of hand--I mean, at all events, the French painting that stands at the beginning of the line of the present tradition. He summoned Leonardo, Andrea del Sarto, Rossi, Primaticcio, and founded the famous Fontainebleau school. Of necessity it was Italianate. It had no Giotto, Masaccio, Raphael behind it. Italian was the best art going; French appreciation was educated and keen; its choice between evolution and adoption was inevitable. It was very much in the position in which American appreciation finds itself to-day. Like our own painters, the French artists of the Renaissance found themselves familiar with masterpieces wholly beyond their power to create, and produced by a foreign people who had enjoyed the incomparable advantage of arriving at their artistic apogee through natural stages of growth, beginning with impulse and culminating in expertness.

The situation had its advantages as well as its drawbacks, certainly. It saved French painting an immense amount of fumbling, of laborious experimentation, of crudity, of failure. But it stamped it with an essential artificiality from which it did not fully recover for over two hundred years, until, insensibly, it had built up its own traditions and gradually brought about its own inherent development. In a word, French painting had an intellectual rather than an emotional origin. Its first practitioners were men of culture rather than of feeling; they were inspired by the artistic, the constructive, the fashioning, rather than the poetic, spirit. And so evident is this inclination in even contemporary French painting--and indeed in all French aesthetic expression--that it cannot be ascribed wholly to the circumstances mentioned. The circumstances themselves need an explanation, and find it in the constitution itself of the French mind, which (owing, doubtless, to other circumstances, but that is extraneous) is fundamentally less imaginative and creative than co-ordinating and constructive.

Naturally thus, when the Italian influence wore itself out, and the Fontaine-bleau school gave way to a more purely national art; when France had definitely entered into her Italian heritage and had learned the lessons that Holland and Flanders had to teach her as well; when, in fine, the art of the modern world began, it was an art of grammar, of rhetoric. Certainly up to the time of Gericault painting in general held itself rather pedantically aloof from poetry. Claude, Chardin, what may be called the illustrated *vers de societe* of the Louis Quinze painters--of Watteau and Fragonard--even Prudhon, did little to change the prevailing color and tone. Claude's art is, in manner, thoroughly classic. His **personal** influence was perhaps first felt by Corot. He stands by himself, at any rate, quite apart. He was the first thoroughly original French painter, if indeed one may not say he was the first thoroughly original modern painter. He has been assigned to both the French and Italian schools--to the latter by Gallophobist critics, however, through a partisanship which in aesthetic matters is ridiculous; there was in his day no Italian school for him to belong to. The truth is that he passed a large part of his life in Italy and that his landscape is Italianate. But more conspicuously still, it is ideal--ideal in the sense intended by Goethe in saying, "There are no landscapes in nature like those of Claude." There are not, indeed. Nature has been transmuted by Claude's alchemy with lovelier results than any other painter--save always Corot, shall I say?--has ever achieved. Witness the pastorals at Madrid, in the Doria Gallery at Rome, the "Dido and AEneas" at Dresden, the sweet and serene superiority of the

National Gallery canvases over the struggling competition manifest in the Turners juxtaposed to them through the unlucky ambition of the great English painter. Mr. Ruskin says that Claude could paint a small wave very well, and acknowledges that he effected a revolution in art, which revolution "consisted mainly in setting the sun in heavens." "Mainly" is delightful, but Claude's excellence consists in his ability to paint visions of loveliness, pictures of pure beauty, not in his skill in observing the drawing of wavelets or his happy thought of painting sunlight. Mr. George Moore observes ironically of Mr. Ruskin that his grotesque depreciation of Mr. Whistler--"the lot of critics" being "to be remembered by what they have failed to understand"--"will survive his finest prose passage." I am not sure about Mr. Whistler. Contemporaries are too near for a perfect critical perspective. But assuredly Mr. Ruskin's failure to perceive Claude's point of view--to perceive that Claude's aim and Stanfield's, say, were quite different; that Claude, in fact, was at the opposite pole from the botanist and the geologist whom Mr. Ruskin's "reverence for nature" would make of every landscape painter--is a failure in appreciation than to have shown which it would be better for him as a critic never to have been born. It seems hardly fanciful to say that the depreciation of Claude by Mr. Ruskin, who is a landscape painter himself, using the medium of words instead of pigments, is, so to speak, professionally unjust.

"Go out, in the springtime, among the meadows that slope from the shores of the Swiss lakes to the roots of their lower mountains. There, mingled with the taller gentians and the white narcissus, the grass grows deep and free; and as you follow the winding mountain paths, beneath arching boughs all veiled and dim with blossom--paths that forever droop and rise over the green banks and mounds sweeping down in scented undulation, steep to the blue water, studded here and there with new-mown heaps, filling the air with fainter sweetness--look up toward the higher hills, where the waves of everlasting green roll silently into their long inlets among the shadows of the pines."

Claude's landscape is not Swiss, but if it were it would awaken in the beholder a very similar sensation to that aroused in the reader of this famous passage. Claude indeed painted landscape in precisely this way. He was perhaps the first--though priority in such matters is trivial beside pre-eminence--who painted ***effects*** instead of ***things***. Light and air were his material, not ponds and rocks and clouds and trees and stretches of plain and mountain outlines. He first generalized the phenomena of inanimate nature, and in this he remains still unsurpassed. But, superficially, his scheme wore the classic aspect, and neither his contemporaries nor his successors, for over two hundred years, discovered the immense value of his point of view, and the puissant charm of his way of rendering nature.

Poussin, however, was the incarnation of the classic spirit, and perhaps the reason why a disinterested foreigner finds it difficult to appreciate the French estimate of him is that no foreigner, however disinterested, can quite appreciate the French appreciation of the classic spirit in and for itself. But when one listens to expressions of admiration for the one French "old master," as one may call Poussin without invidiousness, it is impossible not to scent chauvinism, as one scents it in the German panegyrics of Goethe, for example. He was a very great painter, beyond doubt. And as there were great men before Agamemnon there have been great painters since Raphael and Titian, even since Rembrandt and Velasquez. He had a strenuous personality, moreover. You know a Poussin at once when you see it. But to find the suggestion of the infinite, the Shakespearian touch in his work seems to demand the imaginativeness of M. Victor Cherbuliez. When Mr. Matthew Arnold ventured to remark to Sainte-Beuve that he could not consider Lamartine as a very important poet, Sainte-Beuve replied: "He was important to us." Many critics, among them one severer than Sainte-Beuve, the late Edmond Scherer, have given excellent reasons for Lamartine's absolute as well as relative importance, and perhaps it is a failure in appreciation on our part that is really responsible for our feeling that Poussin is not quite the great master the French deem him. Assuredly he might justifiably apply to himself the "Et-Ego-in-Arcadia" inscription in one of his most famous paintings. And the specific service he performed for French painting and the relative rank he occupies in it ought not to obscure his purely personal qualities, which, if not transcendent, are incontestably elevated and fine.

His qualities, however, are very thoroughly French qualities--poise, rationality, science, the artistic dominating the poetic faculty, and style quite outshining significance and suggestion. He learned all he knew of art, he said, from the Bacchus Torso at Naples. But he was eclectic rather than imitative, and certainly used the material he found in the works of his artistic ancestors as freely and personally as Raphael the frescos of the Baths of Titus, or Donatello the fragments of antique sculpture. From his time on, indeed, French painting dropped its Italian leading-strings. He might often suggest Raphael--and any painter who suggests Raphael inevitably suffers for it--but always with an individual, a native, a French difference, and he is as far removed in spirit and essence from the Fontainebleau school as the French genius itself is from the Italian which presided there. In Poussin, indeed, the French genius first asserts itself in painting. And it asserts itself splendidly in him.

We who ask to be moved as well as impressed, who demand satisfaction of the susceptibility as well as--shall we say rather than?--interest of the intelligence, may feel that for the qualities in which Poussin is lacking those in which he is rich afford no compensation whatever. But I confess that in the presence of even that portion of Poussin's magnificent accomplishment which is spread before one in the Louvre, to wish one's self in the Stanze of the Vatican or in the Sistine Chapel, seems to me an unintelligent sacrifice of one's opportunities.

III

It is a sure mark of narrowness and defective powers of perception to fail to discover the point of view even of what one disesteems. We talk of Poussin, of Louis Quatorze art--as of its revival under David and its continuance in Ingres--of, in general, modern classic art as if it were an art of convention merely; whereas, conventional as it is, its conventionality is--or was, certainly, in the seventeenth century--very far from being pure formulary. It was genuinely expressive of a certain order of ideas intelligently held, a certain set of principles sincerely believed in, a view of art as positive and genuine as the revolt against the tyrannous system into which it developed. We are simply out of sympathy with its aim, its ideal; perhaps, too, for that most frivolous of all reasons because we have grown tired of it.

But the business of intelligent criticism is to be in touch with everything. "Tout comprendre, c'est tout pardonner," as the French ethical maxim has it, may be modified into the true motto of aesthetic criticism, "Tout comprendre, c'est tout justifier." Of course, by "criticism" one does not mean pedagogy, as so many people constantly imagine, nor does justifying everything include bad drawing. But as Lebrun, for example, is not nowadays held up as a model to young painters, and is not to be

accused of bad drawing, why do we so entirely dispense ourselves from compre-
hending him at all? Lebrun is, perhaps, not a painter of enough personal importance
to repay attentive consideration, and historic importance does not greatly concern
criticism. But we pass him by on the ground of his conventionality, without re-
membering that what appears conventional to us was in his case not only sincerity
but aggressive enthusiasm. If there ever was a painter who exercised what creative
and imaginative faculty he had with an absolute gusto, Lebrun did so. He interested
his contemporaries immensely; no painter ever ruled more unrivalled. He fails to
interest us because we have another point of view. We believe in our point of view
and disbelieve in his as a matter of course; and it would be self-contradictory to say,
in the interests of critical catholicity, that in our opinion his may be as sound as our
own. But to say that he has no point of view whatever--to say, in general, that modern classic art is perfunctory and mere formulary--is to be guilty of what has always
been the inherent vice of protestantism in all fields of mental activity.

Nowhere has protestantism exhibited this defect more palpably than in the
course of evolution of schools of painting. Pre-Raphaelitism is perhaps the only
exception, and pre-Raphaelitism was a violent and emotional counter-revolution
rather than a movement characterized by catholicity of critical appreciation. Literary criticism is certainly full of similar intolerance; though when Gautier talks
about Racine, or Zola about "Mes Haines," or Mr. Howells about Scott, the polemic
temper, the temper most opposed to the critical, is very generally recognized. And
in spite of their admirable accomplishment in various branches of literature, these
writers will never quite recover from the misfortune of having preoccupied themselves as critics with the defects instead of the qualities of what is classic. Yet the
protestantism of the successive schools of painting against the errors of their predecessors has something even more crass about it. Contemporary painters and critics thoroughly alive, and fully in the contemporary aesthetic current, so far from
appreciating modern classic art sympathetically, are apt to admire the old masters
themselves mainly on technical grounds, and not at all to enter into their general aesthetic attitude. The feeling of contemporary painters and critics (except, of
course, historical critics) for Raphael's genius is the opposite of cordial. We are out
of touch with the "Disputa," with angels and prophets seated on clouds, with halos
and wings, with such inconsistencies as the "Doge praying" in a picture of the mar-

riage of St. Catherine, with the mystic marriage itself. Raphael's grace of line and suave space-filling shapes are mainly what we think of; the rest we call convention. We are become literal and exacting, addicted to the pedantry of the prescriptive, if not of the prosaic.

Take such a picture as M. Edouard Detaille's "Le Reve," which won him so much applause a few years ago. M. Detaille is an irreproachable realist, and may do what he likes in the way of the materially impossible with impunity. Sleeping soldiers, without a gaiter-button lacking, bivouacking on the ground amid stacked arms whose bayonets would prick; above them in the heavens the clash of contending ghostly armies--wraiths born of the sleepers' dreams. That we are in touch with. No one would object to it except under penalty of being scouted as pitiably literal. Yet the scheme is as thoroughly conventional--that is to say, it is as closely based on hypothesis universally assumed for the moment--as Lebrun's "Triumph of Alexander." The latter is as much a true expression of an ideal as Detaille's picture. It is an ideal now become more conventional, undoubtedly, but it is as clearly an ideal and as clearly genuine. The only point I wish to make is, that Lebrun's painting--Louis Quatorze painting--is not the perfunctory thing we are apt to assume it to be. That is not the same thing, I hope, as maintaining that M. Bouguereau is significant rather than insipid. Lebrun was assuredly not a strikingly original painter. His crowds of warriors bear a much closer resemblance to Raphael's "Battle of Constantine and Maxentius" than the "Transfiguration" of the Vatican does to Giotto's, aside from the important circumstance that the difference in the latter instance shows development, while the former illustrates mainly an enfeebled variation. But there is unquestionably something of Lebrun in Lebrun's work--something typical of the age whose artistic spirit he so completely expressed.

To perceive that Louis Quatorze art is not all convention it is only necessary to remember that Lesueur is to be bracketed with Lebrun. All the sympathy which the Anglo-Saxon temperament withholds from the histrionism of Lebrun is instinctively accorded to his gentle and graceful contemporary, who has been called--*faute de mieux*, of course--the French Raphael. Really Lesueur is as nearly conventional as Lebrun. He has at any rate far less force; and even if we may maintain that he had a more individual point of view, his works are assuredly more monotonous to the scrutinizing sense. It is impossible to recall any one of the famous San Bruno series with any particularity, or, except in subject, to distinguish these in the memory from the sweet and soft "St. Scholastica" in the **Salon Carre**. With more sapience and less sensitiveness, Bouguereau is Lesueur's true successor, to say which is certainly not to affirm a very salient originality of the older painter. He had a great deal of very exquisite feeling for what is refined and elevated, but clearly it is a moral rather than an aesthetic delicacy that he exhibits, and aesthetically he exercises his sweeter and more sympathetic sensibility within the same rigid limits which circumscribe that of Lebrun. He has, indeed, less invention, less imagination, less sense of composition, less wealth of detail, less elaborateness, no greater concentration or sense of effect; and though his color is more agreeable, perhaps, in hue, it gets its tone through the absence of variety rather than through juxtapositions and balances. The truth is, that both equally illustrate the classic spirit, the spirit of their age *par excellence* and of French painting in general, in a supreme degree, though the conformability of the one is positive and of the other passive, so to say; and that neither illustrates quite the subserviency to the conventional which we, who have undoubtedly just as many conventions of our own, are wont to ascribe to them, and to Lebrun in particular.

IV

Fanciful as the Louis Quinze art seems, by contrast with that of Louis Quatorze, it, too, is essentially classic. It is free enough--no one, I think, would deny that--but it is very far from individual in any important sense. It has, to be sure, more personal feeling than that of Lesueur or Lebrun. The artist's susceptibility seems to come to the surface for the first time. Watteau, Fragonard--Fragonard especially, the exquisite and impudent--are as gay, as spontaneous, as careless, as vivacious as Boldini. Boucher's goddesses and cherubs, disporting themselves in graceful abandonment on happily disposed clouds, outlined in cumulus masses against unvarying azure, are as unrestrained and independent of prescription as Monticelli's figures. Lancret, Pater, Nattier, and Van Loo--the very names suggest not merely freedom but a sportive and abandoned license. But in what a narrow round they move! How their imaginativeness is limited by their artificiality! What a talent, what a genius they have for artificiality. It is the era ***par excellence*** of dilettantism, and nothing is less romantic than dilettantism. Their evident feeling--and evidently genuine feeling--is feeling for the factitious, for the manufactured, for what the French call the ***confectionne***. Their romantic quality is to that of the modern Fontainebleau group as the exquisite ***vers de societe*** of Mr. Austin Dobson, say, is to the turbulent yet profound romanticism of Heine or Burns. Every picture painted by them would go as well on a fan as in a frame. All their material is traditional. They simply handle it as ***enfants terribles***. Intellectually speaking, they are painters of a silver age. Of ideas they have almost none. They are as barren of invention in any large sense as if they were imitators instead of, in a sense, the originators of a new phase. Their originality is arrived at rather through exclusion than discovery. They simply drop pedantry and exult in irresponsibility. They are hardly even a school.

Yet they have, one and all, in greater or less degree, that distinct quality of charm which is eternally incompatible with routine. They are as little constructive as the age itself, as anything that we mean when we use the epithet Louis Quinze. Of everything thus indicated one predicates at once unconsciousness, the momentum of antecedent thought modified by the ease born of habit; the carelessness due to having one's thinking done for one and the license of proceeding fancifully, whimsically, even freakishly, once the lines and limits of one's action have been settled by more laborious, more conscientious philosophy than in such circumstances one feels disposed to frame for one's self. There is no break with the Louis Quatorze things, not a symptom of revolt; only, after them the deluge! But out of this very condition of things, and out of this attitude of mind, arises a new art, or rather a new phase of art, essentially classic, as I said, but nevertheless imbued with a character of its own, and this character distinctly charming. Wherein does the charm consist? In two qualities, I think, one of which has not hitherto appeared in French painting, or, indeed, in any art whatever, namely, what we understand by cleverness as a distinct element in treatment--and color. Color is very prominent nowadays in all writing about art, though recently it has given place, in the fashion of the day, to "values" and the realistic representation of natural objects as the painter's proper aim. What precisely is meant by color would be difficult, perhaps, to define. A warmer general tone than is achieved by painters mainly occupied with line and mass is possibly what is oftenest meant by amateurs who profess themselves fond of color. At all events, the Louis Quinze painters, especially Watteau, Fragonard, and Pater--and Boucher has a great deal of the same feeling--were sensitive to that vibration of atmosphere that blends local hues into the *ensemble* that produces tone. The *ensemble* of their tints is what we mean by color. Since the Venetians *this* note had not appeared. They constitute, thus, a sort of romantic interregnum--still very classic, from an intellectual point of view--between the classicism of Lebrun and the still greater severity of David. Nothing in the evolution of French painting is more interesting than this reverberation of Tintoretto and Tiepolo.

By cleverness, as exhibited by the Louis Quinze painters, I do not mean mere technical ability, but something more inclusive, something relating quite as much to attitude of mind as to dexterity of treatment. They conceive as cleverly as they execute. There is a sense of confidence and capability in the way they view, as well as in the way they handle, their light material. They know it thoroughly, and are thoroughly at one with it. And they exploit it with a serene air of satisfaction, as if it were the only material in the world worth handling. Indeed, it is exquisitely adapted to their talent. So little significance has it that one may say it exists merely to be cleverly dealt with, to be represented, distributed, compared, and generally utilized solely with reference to the display of the artist's jaunty skill. It is, one may say, merely the raw material for the production of an effect, and an effect demanding only what we mean by cleverness; no knowledge and love of nature, no prolonged study, no acquaintance with the antique, for example, no philosophy whatever--unless poco-curantism be called a philosophy, which eminently it is not. To be adequate to the requirements--rarely very exacting in any case--made of one, never to show stupidity, to have a great deal of taste and an instinctive feeling for what is elegant and refined, to abhor pedantry and take gayety at once lightly and seriously, and beyond this to take no thought, is to be clever; and in this sense the Louis Quinze painters are the first, as they certainly are the typical, clever artists.

In Louis Quinze art the subject is more than effaced to give free swing to technical cleverness; it is itself contributory to such cleverness, and really a part of it. The artists evidently look on life, as they paint their pictures, as the web whereon to sketch exhibitions of skill in the composition of sensation-provoking combinations--combinations, thus, provoking sensations of the lightest and least substantial kind. When you stand before one of Fragonard's bewitching models, modishly modified into a great--or rather a little--lady, you not only note the color--full of tone on the one hand and of variety on the other, besides exhibiting the happiest selective quality in warm and yet delicate hues and tints; you not only, furthermore, observe the clever touch just poised between suggestion and expression, coquettishly suppressing a detail here, and emphasizing a characteristic there; you feel, in addition, that the entire object floats airily in an atmosphere of cleverness; that it is but a bit, an example, a miniature type of an environment wholly attuned to the note of cleverness--of competence, facility, grace, elegance, and other abstract but not at all abstruse qualities, quite unrelated to what, in any profound sense, at least, is concrete and vitally significant. Artificiality so permeated the Louis Quinze epoch, indeed, that one may say that nature itself was artificial--that is to say, all the nature Louis Quinze painters had to paint; at least all they could have been called upon to think of painting. What a distinction is, after all, theirs! To have created out of nothing, or next to nothing, something charming, and enduringly charming; something of a truly classic inspiration without dependence at bottom on the real and the actual; something as little indebted to facts and things as a fairy tale, and withal marked by such qualities as color and cleverness in so eminent a degree.

The Louis Quinze painters may be said, indeed, to have had the romantic temperament with the classic inspiration. They have audacity rather than freedom, license modified by strict limitation to the lines within which it is exercised. But there can be no doubt that this limitation is more conspicuous in their charmingly irresponsible works than is, essentially speaking, their irresponsibility itself. They never give their imagination free play. Sportive and spontaneous as it appears, it is equally clear that its activities are bounded by conservatory confines. Watteau, born on the Flemish border, is almost an exception. Temperament in him seems constantly on the verge of conquering tradition and environment. Now and then he seems to be on the point of emancipation, and one expects to come upon some work in which he has expressed himself and attested his ideality. But one is as constantly disappointed. His color and his cleverness are always admirable and winning, but his import is perversely--almost bewitchingly--slight. What was he thinking of? one asks, before his delightful canvases; and one's conclusion inevitably is, certainly as near nothing at all as can be consistent with so much charm and so much real power. As to Watteau, one's last thought is of what he would have been in a different aesthetic atmosphere, in an atmosphere that would have stimulated his really romantic temperament to extra-traditional flights, instead of confining it within the inexorable boundaries of classic custom; an atmosphere favorable to the free exercise of his adorable fancy, instead of rigorously insistent on conforming this, so far as might be, to customary canons, and, at any rate, restricting its exercise to material *a la mode*. A little landscape in the La Caze collection in the Louvre, whose romantic and truly poetic feeling agreeably pierces through its elegance, is eloquent of such reflections.

V

With Greuze and Chardin we are supposed to get into so different a sphere of thought and feeling that the change has been called a "return to nature"--that "return to nature" of which we hear so much in histories of literature as well as of the plastic arts. The notion is not quite sound. Chardin is a painter who seems to me, at least, to stand quite apart, quite alone, in the development of French painting, whereas there could not be a more marked instance of the inherence of the classic spirit in the French aesthetic nature than is furnished by Greuze. The first French painter of *genre*, in the full modern sense of the term, the first true interpreter of scenes from humble life--of lowly incident and familiar situations, of broken jars and paternal curses, and buxom girls and precocious children--he certainly is. There is certainly nothing *regence* about him. But the beginning and end of Greuze's art is convention. He is less imaginative, less romantic, less real than the painting his replaced. That was at least a mirror of the ideals, the spirit, the society, of the day. A Louis Quinze fan is a genuine and spontaneous product of a free and elastic aesthetic impulse beside one of his stereotyped sentimentalities.

The truth is, Greuze is as sentimental as a bullfinch, but he has hardly a natural note in his gamut. Nature is not only never his model, she is never his inspiration. He is distinctively a literary painter; but this description is not minute enough. His conventions are those not merely of the *litterateur*, but of the extremely conventional *litterateur*. An artless platitude is really more artificial than a clever paradox; it doesn't even cast a side-light on the natural material with which it deals.

Greuze's **genre** is really a **genre** of his own--his own and that of kindred spirits since. It is as systematic and detached as the art of Poussin. The forms it embodies merely have more natural, more familiar associations. But compare one of his compositions with those of the little Dutch and Flemish masters, for truth, feeling, nature handled after her own suggestions, instead of within limits and on lines imposed upon her from without. By the side of Van Ostade or Brauer, for example, one of Greuze's bits of humble life seems like an academic composition, quite out of touch with its subject, and, except for its art, absolutely lifeless and insipid.

In a word, his choice of subjects, of **genre**, is really no disguise at all of his essential classicality. Both ideally and technically, in the way he conceives and the way he handles his subject, he is only superficially romantic or real. His literature, so to speak, is as conventional as his composition. One may compare him to Hogarth, though both as a moralist and a technician *a longo intervallo*, of course. He is assuredly not to be depreciated. His scheme of color is clear if not rich, his handling is frank if not unctuous or subtly interesting, his composition is careful and clever, and some of his heads are admirably painted--painted with a genuine feeling for quality. But his merits as well as his failings are decidedly academic, and as a romanticist he is really masquerading. He is much nearer to Fragonard than he is to Edouard Frere even.

Chardin, on the other hand, is the one distinguished exception to the general character of French art in the artificial and intellectual eighteenth century. He is as natural as a Dutchman, and as modern as Vollon. As you walk through the French galleries of the Louvre, of all the canvases antedating our own era his are those toward which one feels the most sympathetic attraction, I think. You note at once his individuality, his independence of schools and traditions, his personal point of view, his preoccupation with the object as he perceives it. Nothing is more noteworthy in the history of French art, in the current of which the subordination of the individual genius to the general consensus is so much the rule, than the occasional exception--now of a single man, now of a group of men, destined to become in its turn a school--the occasional accent or interruption of the smooth course of slow development on the lines of academic precedent. Tyrannical as academic precedent is (and nowhere has it been more tyrannical than in French painting) the general interest in aesthetic subjects which a general subscription to academic precedent implies is certainly to be credited with the force and genuineness of the occasional protestant against the very system that has been powerful enough to popularize indefinitely the subject both of subscription and of revolt. Without some such systematic propagandism of the aesthetic cultus as from the first the French Institute has been characterized by, it is very doubtful if, in the complexity of modern society, the interest in aesthetics can ever be made wide enough, universal enough, to spread beyond those immediately and professionally concerned with it. The immense impetus given to this interest by a central organ of authority, that dignifies the subject with which it occupies itself and draws attention to its value and its importance, has, *a priori*, the manifest effect of leading persons to occupy themselves with it, also, who otherwise would never have had their attention drawn to it. It would scarcely be an exaggeration to say, in other words, that but for the Institute there would not be a tithe of the number of names now on the roll of French artists. When art is in the air--and nothing so much as an academy produces this condition--the chances of the production of even an unacademic artist are immensely increased.

So in the midst of the Mignardise of Louis Quinze painting it is only superficially surprising to find a painter of the original force and flavor of Chardin. His wholesome and yet subtle variations from the art *a la mode* of his epoch might have been painted in the Holland of his day, or in our day anywhere that art so good as Chardin's can be produced, so far as subject and moral and technical attitude are concerned. They are, in quite accentuated contra-distinction from the works of Greuze, thoroughly in the spirit of simplicity and directness. One notes in them at once that moral simplicity which predisposes everyone to sympathetic appreciation. The special ideas of his time seem to pass him by unmoved. He has no community of interest with them. While he was painting his still life and domestic genre, the whole fantastic whirl of Louis Quinze society, with its aesthetic standards and accomplishments--accomplishments and standards that imposed themselves everywhere else--was in agitated movement around him without in the least affecting his serene tranquillity, his almost sturdy composure. There can rarely have been such an instance as he affords of an artist's selecting from his environment just those things his own genius needed, and rejecting just what would have hampered or distracted him. He is as sane, as unsentimental, as truthful and unpretending as the most literal and unimaginative Dutchman of his time or before it; but he has also that feeling for style, and that instinct for avoiding the common and unclean which always seem to prevent French painters from "sinking with their subject," as Dutch painters have been said to do. He seems never to let himself go either in the direction of Greuze's literary and sentimental manipulation of his homely material, or in the direction of supine satisfaction with this material, unrelieved and unelevated by an individual point of view, illustrated by the Brauers and Steens and Ostades. One perceives that what he cared for was really art itself, for the aesthetic aspect and significance of the life he painted. Affectionate as his interest in it evidently was, he as evidently thought of its artistic potentialities, its capability of being treated with refinement and delicacy, and of being made to serve the ends of beauty equally well with the conventionally beautiful material of his fan-painting contemporaries. He looked at the world very originally through and over those round, horn-bowed spectacles of his, with a very shrewd and very kindly and sympathetic glance, too; quite untinctured with prejudice or even predisposition. One can read his artistic isolation in his countenance with a very little exercise of fancy.

VI

It is the fashion to think of David as the painter of the Revolution and the Empire. Really he is Louis Seize. Historical critics say that he had no fewer than four styles, but apart from obvious labels they would be puzzled to tell to which of these styles any individual picture of his belongs. He was from the beginning extremely, perhaps absurdly, enamoured of the antique, and we usually associate addiction to the antique with the Revolutionary period. But perhaps politics are slower than the aesthetic movement; David's view of art and practice of painting were fixed unalterably under the reign of philosophism. Philosophism, as Carlyle calls it, is the ruling spirit of his work. Long before the Revolution--in 1774--he painted what is still his most characteristic picture--"The Oath of the Horatii." His art developed and grew systematized under the Republic and the Empire; but Napoleon, whose genius crystallized the elements of everything in all fields of intellectual effort with which he occupied himself, did little but formally "consecrate," in French phrase, the art of the painter of "The Oath of the Horatii" and the originator and designer of the "Fete" of Robespierre's "Etre Supreme." Spite of David's subserviency and that of others, he left painting very much where he found it. And he found it in a state of reaction against the Louis Quinze standards. The break with these, and with everything *regence*, came with Louis Seize, Chardin being a notable exception and standing quite apart from the general drift of the French aesthetic movement; and Greuze being only a pseudo-romanticist, and his work a variant of, rather than re-actionary from, the artificiality of his day. Before painting could "return to nature," before the idea and inspiration of true romanticism could be born, a reaction in the direction of severity after the artificial yet irresponsible riot of the Louis Quinze painters was naturally and logically inevitable. Painting was modified in the same measure with every other expression in the general *recueillement* that followed the extravagance in all social and intellectual fields of the Louis Quinze epoch. But in becoming more chaste it did not become less classical. Indeed, so far as sever-ity is a trait of classicality--and it is only an associated not an essential trait of it--painting became more classical. It threw off its extravagances without swerving from the artificial character of its inspiration. Art in general seemed content with substituting the straight line for the curve--a change from Louis Quinze to Louis Seize that is very familiar even to persons who note the transitions between the two epochs only in the respective furniture of each; a Louis Quinze chair or mirror, for example, having a flowing outline, whereas a Louis Seize equivalent is more rigid and rectilinear.

David is artificial, it is to be pointed out, only in his *ensemble*. In detail he is real enough. And he always has an *ensemble*. His compositions, as compositions, are admirable. They make a total impression, and with a vigor and vividness that belong to few constructed pictures. The canvas is always penetrated with David--illustrates as a whole, and with completeness and comparative flawlessness, his point of view, his conception of the subject. This, of course, is the academic point of view, the academic conception. But, as I say, his detail is surprisingly truthful and studied. His picture--which is always nevertheless a picture--is as inconceivable, as traditional in its inspiration, as factitious as you like; his figures are always sapiently and often happily exact. His portraits are absolutely vital characterizations. And in general his sculptural sense, his self-control, his perfect power of expressing what he deemed worth expressing, are really what are noteworthy in his pictures, far more than their monotonous coloration and the coldness and unreality of the pictures themselves, considered as moving, real, or significant compositions. In admiration of these it is impossible for us nowadays to go as far as even the romanticist, though extremely catholic, Gautier. They leave us cold. We have a wholly different ideal, which in order to interest us powerfully painting must illustrate--an ideal of more pertinence and appositeness to our own moods and manner of thought and feeling.

Ingres, a painter of considerably less force, I think, comes much nearer to doing this. He is more elastic, less devoted to system. Without being as free, as sensitive to impressions as we like to see an artist of his powers, he escapes pedantry. His subject is not "The Rape of the Sabines," but "The Apotheosis of Homer," academic but not academically fatuitous. To follow the inspiration of the Vatican Stanze in the selection and treatment of ideal subjects is to be far more closely in touch with contemporary feeling as to what is legitimate and proper in imaginative painting, than to pictorialize an actual event with a systematic artificiality and conformity to abstractions that would surely have made the sculptor of the Trajan column smile. Yet I would rather have "The Rape of the Sabines" within visiting distance than "The Apotheosis of Homer." It is better, at least solider, painting. The painter, however dominated by his theory, is more the master of its illustration than Ingres is of the justification of his admiration for Raphael. The "Homer" attempts more, but it is naturally not as successful in getting as effective a unity out of its greater complexity. It is in his less ambitious pictures that the genius of Ingres is unmistakably evident--his heads, his single figures, his exquisite drawings almost in outline. His "Odalisque" of the Louvre is not as forceful as David's portrait of Madame Recamier, but it is a finer thing. I should like the two to have changed subjects in this instance. His "Source" is beautifully drawn and modelled. In everything he did distinction is apparent. Inferior assuredly to David when he attempted the grand style, he had a truer feeling for the subtler qualities of style itself. All his works are linearly beautiful demonstrations of his sincerity--his sanity indeed--in proclaiming that drawing is "the probity of art."

With a few contemporary painters and critics, whose specific penetration is sometimes in curious contrast with their imperfect catholicity, he has recently

come into vogue again, after having been greatly neglected since the romantic outburst. But he belongs completely to the classic epoch. Neither he nor his refined
and sympathetic pupil, Flandrin, did aught to pave the way for the modern movement. Intimations of the shifting point of view are discoverable rather in a painter
of far deeper poetic interest than either, spite of Ingres's refinement and Flandrin's
elevation--in Prudhon. Prudhon is the link between the last days of the classic
supremacy and the rise of romanticism. Like Claude, like Chardin, he stands somewhat apart; but he has distinctly the romantic inspiration, constrained and regular-
ized by classic principles of taste. He is the French Correggio in far more precise
parallelism than Lesueur is the French Raphael. With a grace and lambent color all
his own--a beautiful mother-of-pearl and opalescent tone underlying his exquisite
violets and graver hues; a color-scheme, on the one hand, and a sense of design in
line and mass more suave and graceful than anything since the great Italians, on the
other--he recalls the lovely chiaro-oscuro of the exquisite Parmesan as it is recalled
in no other modern painter. Occupying, as incontestably he does, his own niche
in the pantheon of painters, he nevertheless illustrates most distinctly and unmistakably the slipping away of French painting from classic formulas as well as from
classic extravagance, and the tendency to new ideals of wider reach and greater
tolerance--of more freedom, spontaneity, interest in "life and the world"--of a de-
finitive break with the contracting and constricting forces of classicism. During its
next period, and indeed down to the present day, French painting will preserve the
essence of its classic traditions, variously modified from decade to decade, but never
losing the quality in virtue of which what is French is always measurably the most
classic thing going; but of this next period certainly Prudhon is the precursor, who,
with all his classic serenity, presages its passion for "storms, clouds, effusion, and
relief."

II

ROMANTIC PAINTING

I

When we come to Scott after Fielding, says Mr. Stevenson, "we become suddenly conscious of the background." The remark contains an admirable characterization of romanticism; as distinguished from classicism, romanticism is consciousness of the background. With Gros, Gericault, Paul Huet, Michel, Delacroix, French painting ceased to be abstract and impersonal. Instead of continuing the classic detachment, it became interested, curious, and catholic. It broadened its range immensely, and created its effect by observing the relations of its objects to their environment, of its figures to the landscape, of its subjects to their suggestions even in other spheres of thought; Delacroix, Marilhat, Decamps, Fromentin, in painting the aspect of Orientalism, suggested, one may almost say, its sociology. For the abstractions of classicism, its formula, its fastidious system of arriving at perfection by exclusions and sacrifices, it substituted an enthusiasm for the concrete and the actual; it revelled in natural phenomena. Gautier was never more definitely the exponent of romanticism than in saying "I am a man for whom the visible world exists." To lines and curves and masses and their relations in composition, succeeds as material for inspiration and reproduction the varied spectacle of the external world. With the early romanticists it may be said that for the first time the external world "swims into" the painter's "ken." But, above all, in them the element of personality first appears in French painting with anything like general acceptance and as the characteristic of a group, a school, rather than as an isolated exception here and there, such as Claude or Chardin. The "point of view" takes the place of conformity to a standard. The painter expresses himself instead of endeavoring to realize an extraneous and impersonal ideal. What he himself personally thinks, how he himself personally feels, is what we read in his works.

It is true that, rightly understood, the romantic epoch is a period of evolution, and orderly evolution at that, if we look below the surface, rather than of systematic defiance and revolt. It is true that it recast rather than repudiated its inheritance of tradition. Nevertheless there has never been a time when the individual felt himself so free, when every man of any original genius felt so keenly the exhilaration of independence, when the "schools" of painting exercised less tyranny and, indeed, counted for so little. If it be exact to speak of the "romantic school" at all, it should be borne in mind that its adherents were men of the most marked and diverse individualities ever grouped under one standard. The impressionists, perhaps, apart, individuality is often spoken of as the essential characteristic of the painters of the present day. But beside the outburst of individuality at the beginning of the romantic epoch, much of the painting of the present day seems both monotonous and eccentric--the variation of its essential monotony, that is to say, being somewhat labored and express in comparison with the spontaneous multifariousness of the epoch of Delacroix and Decamps. In the decade between 1820 and 1830, at all events, notwithstanding the strength of the academic tradition, painting was free from the thraldom of system, and the imagination of its practitioners was not challenged and circumscribed by the criticism that is based upon science. Not only in the painter's freedom in his choice of subject, but in his way of treating it, in the way in which he "takes it," is the revolution--or, as I should be inclined to say, rather, the evolution--shown. And as what we mean by personality is, in general, made up far more of emotion than of mind--there being room for infinitely more variety in feeling than in mental processes among intelligent agents--it is natural to find the French romantic painters giving, by contrast with their predecessors, such free swing to personal feeling that we may almost sum up the origin of the romantic movement in French painting in saying that it was an ebullition of emancipated emotion. And, to go a step farther, we may say that, as nothing is so essential to poetry as feeling, we meet now for the first time with the poetic element as an inspiring motive and controlling force.

The romantic painters were, however, by no means merely emotional. They were mainly imaginative. And in painting, as in literature, the great change wrought by romanticism consisted in stimulating the imagination instead of merely satisfying the sense and the intellect. The main idea ceased to be as obviously accentuated, and its natural surroundings were given their natural place; there was less direct statement and more suggestion; the artist's effort was expended rather upon perfecting the *ensemble*, noting relations, taking in a larger circle; a suggested complexity of moral elements took the place of the old simplicity, whose multifariousness was almost wholly pictorial. Instead of a landscape as a tapestry background to a Holy Family, and having no pertinence but an artistic one, we have Corot's "Orpheus."

II

Gericault and Delacroix are the great names inscribed at the head of the romantic roll. They will remain there. And the distinction is theirs not as awarded by the historical estimate; it is personal. In the case of Gericault perhaps one thinks a little of "the man and the moment" theory. He was, it is true, the first romantic painter--at any rate the first notable romantic painter. His struggles, his steadfastness, his success--pathetically posthumous--have given him an honorable eminence. His example of force and freedom exerted an influence that has been traced not only in the work of Delacroix, his immediate inheritor, but in that of the sculptor Rude, and even as far as that of Millet--to all outward appearance so different in inspiration from that of his own tumultuous and dramatic genius. And as of late years we look on the stages of any evolution as less dependent on individuals than we used to, doubtless just as Luther was confirmed and supported on his way to the Council at Worms by the people calling on him from the house-tops not to deny the truth, Gericault was sustained and stimulated in the face of official obloquy by a more or less considerable aesthetic movement of which he was really but the leader and exponent. But his fame is not dependent upon his revolt against the Institute, his influence upon his successors, or his incarnation of an aesthetic movement. It rests on his individual accomplishment, his personal value, the abiding interest of his pictures. "The Raft of the Medusa" will remain an admirable and moving creation, a masterpiece of dramatic vigor and vivid characterization, of wide and deep human interest and truly panoramic grandeur, long after its contemporary interest and historic importance have ceased to be thought of except by the aesthetic antiquarian. "The Wounded Cuirassier" and the "Chasseur of the Guard" are not documents of aesthetic history, but noble expressions of artistic sapience and personal feeling.

What, I think, is the notable thing about both Gericault and Delacroix, however, as exponents, as the initiators, of romanticism, is the way in which they restrained the impetuous temperament they share within the confines of a truly classic reserve. Closely considered, they are not the revolutionists they seemed to the official classicism of their day. Not only do they not base their true claims to enduring fame upon a spirit of revolt against official and academic art--a spirit essentially negative and nugatory, and never the inspiration of anything permanently puissant and attractive--but, compared with their successors of the present day, in whose works individual preference and predilection seem to have a swing whose very freedom and irresponsible audacity extort admiration--compared with the confident temerariousness of what is known as *modernite*, their self-possession and sobriety seem their most noteworthy characteristics. Compared with the "Bar at the Folies-Bergere," either the "Raft of the Medusa" or the "Convulsionists of Tangiers" is a classic production. And the difference is not at all due to the forty years' accretion of Protestantism which Manet represents as compared with the early romanticists. It is due to a complete difference in attitude. Gericault imbued himself with the inspiration of the Louvre. Delacroix is said always to have made a sketch from the old masters or the antique a preliminary to his own daily work. So far from flaunting tradition, they may be said to have, in their own view, restored it; so far from posing as apostles of innovation, they may almost be accused of "harking back"--of steeping themselves in what to them seemed best and finest and most authoritative in art, instead of giving a free rein to their own unregulated emotions and conceptions.

Gericault died early and left but a meagre product. Delacroix is *par excellence* the representative of the romantic epoch. And both by the mass and the quality of his work he forms a true connecting link between the classic epoch and the modern--in somewhat the same way as Prudhon does, though more explicitly and on the other side of the line of division. He represents culture--he knows art as well as he loves nature. He has a feeling for what is beautiful as well as a knowledge of what is true. He is pre-eminently and primarily a colorist--he is, in fact, the introducer of color as a distinct element in French painting after the pale and bleak reaction from the Louis Quinze decorativeness. His color, too, is not merely the prismatic coloration of what had theretofore been mere chiaro-oscuro; it is original and personal to such a degree that it has never been successfully imitated since his day. Withal, it is apparently simplicity itself. Its hues are apparently the primary ones, in the main. It depends upon no subtleties and refinements of tints for its effectiveness. It is significant that the absorbed and affected Rossetti did not like it; it is too frank and clear and open, and shows too little evidence of the morbid brooding and hysterical forcing of an arbitrary and esoteric note dear to the English pre-Raphaelites. It attests a delight in color, not a fondness for certain colors, hues, tints--a difference perfectly appreciable to either an unsophisticated or an educated sense. It has a solidity and strength of range and vibration combined with a subtle sensitiveness, and, as a result of the fusion of the two, a certain splendor that recalls Saracenic decoration. And with this mastery of color is united a combined firmness and expressiveness of design that makes Delacroix unique by emphasizing his truly classic subordination of informing enthusiasm to a severe and clearly perceived ideal--an ideal in a sense exterior to his purely personal expression. In a word, his chief characteristic--and it is a supremely significant trait in the representative painter of romanticism--is a poetic imagination tempered and trained by culture and refinement. When his audacities and enthusiasms are thought of, the directions in his will for his tomb should be remembered too: "Il n'y sera place ni embleme, ni buste, ni statue; mon tombeau sera copie tres exactement sur l'antique, ou Vignoles ou Palladio, avec des saillies tres prononcees, contrairement a tout ce qui se fait aujourd'hui en architecture." "Let there be neither emblem, bust, nor statue on my tomb, which shall be copied very scrupulously after the antique, either Vignola or Palladio, with prominent projections, contrary to everything done to-day in architecture." In a sense all Delacroix is in these words.

III

Delacroix's color deepens into an almost musical intensity occasionally in De-camps, whose oriental landscapes and figures, far less important intellectually, far less **magistrales** in conception, have at times, one may say perhaps without being too fanciful, a truly symphonic quality that renders them unique. "The Suicide" is like a chord on a violin. But it is when we come to speak of the "Fontainebleau Group," in especial, I think, that the aesthetic susceptibility characteristic of the latter half of the nineteenth century feels, to borrow M. Taine's introduction to his lectures on "The Ideal in Art," that the subject is one only to be treated in poetry.

Of the noblest of all so-called "schools," Millet is perhaps the most popular member. His popularity is in great part, certainly, due to his literary side, to the sentiment which pervades, which drenches, one may say, all his later work--his work after he had, on overhearing himself characterized as a painter of naked wom-en, betaken himself to his true subject, the French peasant. A literary, and a very powerful literary side, Millet undoubtedly has; and instead of being a weakness in him it is a power. His sentimental appeal is far from being surplusage, but, as is not I think popularly appreciated, it is subordinate, and the fact of its subordination gives it what potency it has. It is idle to deny this potency, for his portrayal of the French peasant in his varied aspects has probably been as efficient a characteriza-tion as that of George Sand herself. But, if a moral instead of an aesthetic effect had been Millet's chief intention, we may be sure that it would have been made far less incisively than it has been. Compare, for example, his peasant pictures with those of the almost purely literary painter Jules Breton, who has evidently chosen his field for its sentimental rather than its pictorial value, and whose work is, perhaps accordingly, by contrast with Millet's, noticeably external and superficial even on the literary side. When Millet ceased to deal in the Correggio manner with Cor-reggiesque subjects, and devoted himself to the material that was really native to him, to his own peasant genius--whatever he may have thought about it himself, he did so because he could treat this material **pictorially** with more freedom and less artificiality, with more zest and enthusiasm, with a deeper sympathy and a more intimate knowledge of its artistic characteristics, its pictorial potentialities. He is, I think, as a painter, a shade too much preoccupied with this material, he is a little too philosophical in regard to it, his pathetic struggle for existence exaggerated his sentimental affiliations with it somewhat, he made it too exclusively his subject, perhaps. We gain, it may be, at his expense. With his artistic gifts he might have been more fortunate, had his range been broader. But in the main it is his pictorial handling of this material, with which he was in such acute sympathy, that distinguishes his work, and that will preserve its fame long after its humanitarian and sentimental appeal has ceased to be as potent as it now is--at the same time that it has itself enforced this appeal in the subordinating manner I have suggested. When he was asked his intention, in his picture of a maimed calf borne away on a litter by two men, he said it was simply to indicate the sense of weight in the muscular movement and attitude of the bearers' arms.

His great distinction, in fine, is artistic. His early painting of conventional subjects is not without significance in its witness to the quality of his talent. Another may paint French peasants all his life and never make them permanently interesting, because he has not Millet's admirable instinct and equipment as a painter. He is a superb colorist, at times--always an enthusiastic one; there is something almost unregulated in his delight in color, in his fondness for glowing and resplendent tone. No one gets farther away from the academic grayness, the colorless chiaro-oscuro of the conventional painters. He runs his key up and loads his canvas, occasionally, in what one may call not so much barbaric as uncultivated and elementary fashion. He cares so much for color that sometimes, when his effect is intended to be purely atmospheric, as in the "Angelus," he misses its justness and fitness, and so, in insisting on color, obtains from the color point of view itself an infelicitous--a colored-- result. Occasionally he bathes a scene in yellow mist that obscures all accentuations and play of values. But always his feeling for color betrays him a painter rather than a moralist. And in composition he is, I should say, even more distinguished. His composition is almost always distinctly elegant. Even in so simple a scheme as that of "The Sower," the lines are as fine as those of a Raphael. And the way in which balance is preserved, masses are distributed, and an organic play of parts related to each other and each to the sum of them is secured, is in all of his large works so salient an element of their admirable excellence, that, to those who appreciate it, the dependence of his popularity upon the sentimental suggestion of the raw material with which he dealt seems almost grotesque. In his line and mass and the relations of these in composition, there is a severity, a restraint, a conformity to tradition, however personally felt and individually modified, that evince a strong classic strain in this most unacademic of painters. Millet was certainly an original genius, if there ever was one. In spite of, and in open hostility to, the popular and conventional painting of his day, he followed his own bent and went his own way. Better, perhaps, than any other painter, he represents absolute emancipation from the prescribed, from routine and formulary. But it would be a signal mistake to fail to see, in the most characteristic works of this most personal representative of romanticism, that subordination of the individual whim and isolated point of view to what is accepted, proven, and universal, which is essentially what we mean by the classic attitude. One may almost go so far as to say, considering its reserve, its restraint and poise, its sobriety and measure, its quiet and composure, its subordination of individual feeling to a high sense of artistic decorum, that, romantic as it is, unacademic as it is, its most incontestable claim to permanence is the truly classic spirit which, however modified, inspires and infiltrates it. Beside some of the later manifestations of individual genius in French painting, it is almost academic.

In Corot, anyone, I suppose, can see this note, and it would be surplusage to insist upon it. He is the ideal classic-romantic painter, both in temperament and in practice. Millet's subject, not, I think, his treatment--possibly his wider range-- makes him seem more deeply serious than Corot, but he is not essentially as nearly unique. He is unrivalled in his way, but Corot is unparalleled. Corot inherits the tradition of Claude; his motive, like Claude's, is always an effect, and, like Claude's, his means are light and air. But his effect is a shade more impalpable, and his means are at once simpler and more subtle. He gets farther away from the phenomena which are the elements of his *ensemble*, farther than Claude, farther than anyone. His touch is as light as the zephyr that stirs the diaphanous drapery of his trees. Beside it Claude's has a suspicion, at least, of unctuousness. It has a pure, crisp, vibrant accent, quite without analogue in the technic of landscape painting. Taking technic in its widest sense, one may speak of Corot's shortcomings--not, I think, of his failures. It would be difficult to mention a modern painter more uniformly successful in attaining his aim, in expressing what he wishes to express, in conveying his impression, communicating his sensations.

That a painter of his power, a man of the very first rank, should have been content--even placidly content--to exercise it within a range by no means narrow, but plainly circumscribed, is certainly witness of limitation. "Delacroix is an eagle, I am only a skylark," he remarked once, with his characteristic cheeriness. His range is not, it is true, as circumscribed as is generally supposed outside of France. Outside of France his figure-painting, for example, is almost unknown. We see chiefly variations of his green and gray arbored pastoral--now idyllic, now heroic, now full of freshness, the skylark quality, now of grave and deep harmonies and wild, sweet notes of transitory suggestion. Of his figures we only know those shifting shapes that blend in such classic and charming manner with the glades and groves of his landscapes. Of his "Hagar in the Wilderness," his "St. Jerome," his "Flight into Egypt," his "Democritus," his "Baptism of Christ," with its nine life-size figures, who, outside of France, has even heard? How many foreigners know that he painted what are called architectural subjects delightfully, and even *genre* with zest?

But compared with his landscape, in which he is unique, it is plain that he excels nowhere else. The splendid display of his works in the Centenaire Exposition of the great World's Fair of 1889, was a revelation of his range of interest rather than of his range of power. It was impossible not to perceive that, surprising as were his essays in other fields to those who only knew him as a landscape painter, he was essentially and integrally a painter of landscape, though a painter of landscape who had taken his subject in a way and treated it in a manner so personal as to be really unparalleled. Outside of landscape his interest was clearly not real. In his other works one notes a certain *debonnaire* irresponsibility. He pursued nothing seriously but out-of-doors, its vaporous atmosphere, its crisp twigs and graceful branches, its misty distances and piquant accents, what Thoreau calls its inaudible panting. His true theme, lightly as he took it, absorbed him; and no one of any sensitiveness can ever regret it. His powers, following the indication of his true temperament, his most genuine inspiration, are concentrated upon the very finest thing imaginable in landscape painting; as, indeed, to produce as they have done the finest landscape in the history of art, they must have been.

There are, however, two things worth noting in Corot's landscape, beyond the mere fact that, better even than Rousseau, he expresses the essence of landscape, dwells habitually among its inspirations, and is its master rather than its servant. One is the way in which he poetizes, so to speak, the simplest stretches of sward and clumps of trees, and long clear vistas across still ponds, with distances whose accents are pricked out with white houses and yellow cows and placid fishers and ferrymen in red caps, seen in glimpses through curtains of sparse, feathery leafage- -or peoples woodland openings with nymphs and fawns, silhouetted against the sunset glow, or dancing in the cool gray of dusk. A man of no reading, having only the elements of an education in the general sense of the term, his instinctive sense for what is refined was so delicate that we may say of his landscapes that, had the Greeks left any they would have been like Corot's. And this classic and cultivated effect he secured not at all, or only very incidentally, through the force of association, by dotting his hillsides and vaporous distances with bits of classic architecture, or by summing up his feeling for the Dawn in a graceful figure of Orpheus greeting with extended gesture the growing daylight, but by a subtle interpenetration of sensuousness and severity resulting in precisely the sentiment fitly characterized by the epithet classic. The other trait peculiar to Corot's representation of nature and expression of himself is his color. No painter ever exhibited, I think, quite such a sense of refinement in so narrow a gamut. Green and gray, of course, predominate and set the key, but he has an interestingly varied palette on the hither side of splendor whose subtleties are capable of giving exquisite pleasure. Never did anyone use tints with such positive force. Tints with Corot have the vigor and vibration of positive colors--his lilacs, violets, straw-colored hues, his almost Quakerish coquetry with drabs and slates and pure clear browns, the freshness and bloom he imparted to his tones, the sweet and shrinking wild flowers with which as a spray he sprinkled his humid dells and brook margins. But Corot's true distinction--what gives him his unique position at the very head of landscape art, is neither his color, delicate and interesting as his color is, nor his classic serenity harmonizing with, instead of depending upon, the chance associations of architecture and mythology with which now and then he decorates his landscapes; it is the blithe, the airy, the truly spiritual way in which he gets farther away than anyone from both the actual pigment that is his instrument, and from the phenomena that are the objects of his expression--his ethereality, in a word. He has communicated his sentiment almost without material, one may say, so ethereally independent of their actual analogues is the interest of his trees and sky and stretch of sward. This sentiment, thus mysteriously triumphant over color or form, or other sensuous charm, which nevertheless are only subtly subordinated, and by no manner of means treated lightly or inadequately, is as exalted as any that has in our day been expressed in any manner. Indeed, where, outside of the very highest poetry of the century, can one get the same sense of elation, of aspiring delight, of joy unmixed with regret--since "the splendor of truth" which Plato defined beauty to be, is more animating and consoling than the "weary weight of all this unintelligible world," is depressing to a spirit of lofty seriousness and sanity?

*   *   *   *   *

Dupre and Diaz are the decorative painters of the Fontainebleau group. They are, of modern painters, perhaps the nearest in spirit to the old masters, pictorially speaking. They are rarely in the grand style, though sometimes Dupre is restrained enough to emulate if not to achieve its sobriety. But they have the ***bel air***, and belong to the aristocracy of the painting world. Diaz, especially, has almost invariably the patrician touch. It lacks the exquisiteness of Monticelli's, in which there is that curiously elevated detachment from the material and the real that the Italians--and the Provencal painter's inspiration and method, as well as his name and lineage, suggest an Italian rather than a French association--exhibit far oftener than the French. But Diaz has a larger sweep, a saner method. He is never eccentric, and he has a dignity that is Iberian, though he is French rather than Spanish on his aesthetic side, and at times is as conservative as Rousseau--without, however, reaching Rousseau's lofty simplicity except in an occasional happy stroke. Both he and Dupre are primarily colorists. Dupre sees nature through a prism. Diaz's groups of dames and gallants have a jewel-like aspect; they leave the same impression as a tangle of ribbons, a bunch of exotic flowers, a heap of gems flung together with the felicity of haphazard. In general, and when they are in most completely characteristic mood, it is not the sentiment of nature that one gets from the work of either painter. It is not even ***their*** sentiment of nature--the emotion aroused in their susceptibilities by natural phenomena. What one gets is their personal feeling for color and design-

-their decorative quality, in a word.

The decorative painter is he to whom what is called "subject," even in its least restricted sense and with its least substantial suggestions, is comparatively indifferent. Nature supplies him with objects; she is not in any intimate degree his subject. She is the medium through which, rather than the material of which, he creates his effects. It is her potentialities of color and design that he seeks, or at any rate, of all her infinitely numerous traits, it is her hues and arabesques that strike him most forcibly. He is incurious as to her secrets and calls upon her aid to interpret his own, but he is so independent of her, if he be a decorative painter of the first rank--a Diaz or a Dupre--that his rendering of her, his picture, would have an agreeable effect, owing to its design or color or both, if it were turned upside down. Decorative painting in this sense may easily be carried so far as to seem incongruous and inept, in spite of its superficial attractiveness. The peril that threatens it is whim and freak. Some of Monticelli's, some of Matthew Maris's pictures, illustrate the exaggeration of the decorative impulse. After all, a painter must get his effect, whatever it be and however it may shun the literal and the exact, by rendering things with pigments. And some of the decorative painters only escape things by obtruding pigments, just as the ***trompe-l'oeil*** or optical illusion painters get away from pigments by obtruding things. It is the distinction of Diaz and Dupre that they avoid this danger in most triumphant fashion. On the contrary, they help one to see the decorative element in nature, in "things," to a degree hardly attained elsewhere since the days of the great Venetians. Their predilection for the decorative element is held in leash by the classic tradition, with its reserve, its measure, its inculcation of sobriety and its sense of security. Dupre paints Seine sunsets and the edge of the forest at Fontainebleau, its "long mysterious reaches fed with moonlight," in a way that conveys the golden glow, the silvery gleam, the suave outline of spreading leafage, and the massive density of mysterious boscage with the force of an almost abstract acuteness. Does nature look like this? Who knows? But in this semblance, surely, she appeared to Dupre's imagination. And doubtless Diaz saw the mother-of-pearl tints in the complexion of his models, and is not to be accused of artificiality, but to be credited with a true sincerity of selection in juxtaposing his soft corals and carnations and gleaming topaz, amethyst, and sapphire hues. The most exacting literalist can hardly accuse them of solecism in their rendering of nature, true as it is that their decorative sense is so strong as to lead them to impose on nature their own sentiment instead of yielding themselves to absorption in ***hers***, and thus, in harmonious and sympathetic concert with her, like Claude and Corot, Rousseau and Daubigny, interpreting her subtle and supreme significance.

*   *   *   *   *

Rousseau carried the fundamental principle of the school farther than the others--with him interest, delight in, enthusiasm for nature became absorption in her. Whereas other men have loved nature, it has been acutely remarked, Rousseau was in love with her. It was felicitously of him, rather than of Dupre or Corot, that the naif peasant inquired, "Why do you paint the tree; the tree is there, is it not?" And never did nature more royally reward allegiance to her than in the sustenance and inspiration she furnished for Rousseau's genius. You feel the point of view in his picture, but it is apparently that of nature herself as well as his own. It is not the less personal for this. On the contrary, it is extremely personal, and few pictures are as individual, as characteristic. Occasionally Diaz approaches him, as I have said, but only in the very happiest and exceptional moments, when the dignity of nature as well as her charm seems specially to impress and impose itself upon the less serious painter. But Rousseau's selection seems instinctive and not sought out. He knows the secret of nature's pictorial element. He is at one with her, adopts her suggestions so cordially and works them out with such intimate sympathy and harmoniousness, that the two forces seem reciprocally to reinforce each other, and the result gains many fold in power from their subtle co-operation. His landscapes have in this way a Wordsworthian directness, simplicity, and severity. They are not troubled and dramatic like Turner's. They are not decorative like Dupre's, they have not the solemn sentiment of Daubigny's, or the airy aspiration and fairy-like blitheness of Corot's. But there is in them "all breathing human passion;" and at times, as in "Le Givre," they rise to majesty and real grandeur because they are impregnated with the sentiment, as well as are records of the phenomena, of nature, and one may say of Rousseau, paraphrasing Mr. Arnold's remark about Wordsworth, that nature seems herself to take the brush out of his hand and to paint for him "with her own bare, sheer, penetrating power." Rousseau, however, is French, and in virtue of his nativity exhibits always what Wordsworth's treatment of nature exhibits only occasionally, namely, the Gallic gift of style. It is rarely as felicitous as in Corot, in every detail of whose every work, one may almost say, its informing, co-ordinating, elevating influence is distinctly to be perceived; but it is always present as a factor, as a force dignifying and relieving from all touch, all taint of the commonness that is so often inseparably associated with art whose absorption in nature is listlessly unthinking instead of enthusiastic and alert. In Rousseau, too, in a word, we have the classic strain, as at least a psychological element, and note as one source of his power his reserve and restraint, his perfect self-possession.

In Daubigny a similar attitude toward nature is obvious, but with a sensible difference. Affection for, rather than absorption in her, is his inspiration. Daubigny stands somewhat apart from the Fontainebleau group, with whom nevertheless he is popularly and properly associated, for though he painted Normandy mainly, he was spiritually of the Barbizon kindred. He stands, however, somewhat apart from French painting in general, I think. There is less style, more sentiment, more poetry in his landscapes than in those of his countrymen who are to be compared with him. Beyond what is admirable in them there is something attaching as well. He drew and engraved a good deal, as well as painted. He did not concentrate his powers enough, perhaps, to make as signal and definite a mark as otherwise he might have done. He is a shade desultory, and too spontaneous to be systematic. One must be systematic to reach the highest point, even in the least material spheres. But never have the grave and solemn aspects of landscape found a sweeter and serener spirit to interpret them. In some of his pictures there is a truly religious feeling. His frankness recalls Constable's, but it is more distinguished in being more spiritual. He has not Diaz's elegance, nor Corot's witchery, nor Rousseau's power, but nature is more mysteriously, more mystically significant to him, and sets a deeper chord vibrating within him. He is a sensitive instrument on which she plays, rather than a magician who wins her secrets, or an observer whose generalizing imagination she sets in motion. The design of some of his important works, notably that of his last *Salon* picture, is very distinguished, and in one of his large canvases representing a road like that from Barbizon through the level plain to Chailly, there is the spirit and sentiment of all the summer evenings that ever were. But he has distinctly less power than the strict Fontainebleau group. He has, in force, less affinity with them than Troyon has, whose force is often magnificent, and whose landscape is so sweet, often, and often so strong as well, that one wonders a little at his fondness for cattle--in spite of the way in which he justifies it by being the first of cattle painters. And neither Daubigny nor Troyon, nor, indeed, Rousseau himself, often reaches in dramatic grandeur the lofty landscape of Michel, who, with Paul Huet (the latter in a more strictly historical sense) were so truly the forerunners and initiators of the romantic landscape movement, both in sentiment and chronology, in spite of their Dutch tradition, as to make the common ascription of its debt to Constable, whose aid was so cordially welcomed in the famous Salon of 1824, a little strained.

IV

But quite aside from the group of poetic painters which stamped its impress so deeply upon the romantic movement at the outset, that to this day it is Delacroix and Millet, Decamps and Corot whom we think of when we think of the movement itself, the classic tradition was preserved all through the period of greatest stress and least conformity by painters of great distinction, who, working under the romantic inspiration and more or less according to what may be called romantic methods, nevertheless possessed the classic temperament in so eminent a degree that to us their work seems hardly less academic than that of the Revolution and the Empire. Not only Ingres, but Delaroche and Ary Scheffer, painted beside Gericault and Delacroix. Ary Scheffer was an eloquent partisan of romanticism, yet his "Dante and Beatrice" and his "Temptation of Christ" are admirable only from the academic point of view. Delaroche's "Hemicycle" and his many historical tableaux are surely in the classic vein, however free they may seem in subject and treatment by contrast with the works of David and Ingres. They leave us equally cold, at all events, and in the same way--for the same reason. They betray the painter's preoccupation with art rather than with nature. They do, in truth, differ widely from the works which they succeeded, but the difference is not temperamental. They suggest the French phrase, *plus ca change, plus c'est la meme chose*. Gerome, for example, feels the exhilaration of the free air of romanticism fanning his enthusiasm. He does not confine himself, as, born a decade or two earlier, certainly he would have done, to classic subject. He follows Decamps and Marilhat to the Orient, which he paints with the utmost freedom, so far as the choice of theme is concerned--descending even to the *danse du ventre* of a Turkish cafe. He paints historical pictures with a realism unknown before his day. He is almost equally famous in the higher class of *genre* subjects. But throughout everything he does it is easy to perceive the academic point of view, the classic temperament. David assuredly would never have chosen one of Gerome's themes; but had he chosen it, he would have treated it in much the same way. Allowance made for the difference in time, in general feeling of the aesthetic environment, the change in ideas as to what was fit subject for representation and fitting manner of treating the same subject, it is hardly an exaggeration to say that Ingres would have sincerely applauded Gerome's "Cleopatra" issuing from the carpet roll before Caesar. And if he failed to perceive the noble dramatic power in such a work as the "Ave, Caesar, morituri te salutant," his failure would nowadays, at least among intelligent amateurs, be ascribed to an intolerance which it is one of the chief merits of the romantic movement to have adjudged absurd.

It is a source of really aesthetic satisfaction to see everything that is attempted as well done as it is in the works of such painters as Bouguereau and Cabanel. Of course the feeling that denies them large importance is a legitimate one. The very excellence of their technic, its perfect adaptedness to the motive it expresses, is, considering the insignificance of the motive, subject for criticism; inevitably it partakes of the futility of its subject-matter. Of course the personal value of the man, the mind, behind any plastic expression is, in a sense, the measure of the expression itself. If it be a mind interested in "pouncet-box" covers, in the pictorial setting forth of themes whose illustration most intimately appeals to the less cultivated and more rudimentary appreciation of fine art--as indisputably the Madonnas and Charities and Oresteses and Bacchus Triumphs of M. Bouguereau do--one may very well dispense himself from the duty of admiring its productions. Life is short, and more important things, things of more significant import, demand attention. The grounds on which the works of Bouguereau and Cabanel are admired are certainly insufficient. But they are experts in their sphere. What they do could hardly be better done. If they appeal to a *bourgeois*, a philistine ideal of beauty, of interest, they do it with a perfection that is pleasing in itself. No one else does it half so well. To minds to which they appeal at all, they appeal with the force of finality; for these they create as well as illustrate the type of what is admirable and lovely. It is as easy to account for their popularity as it is to perceive its transitory quality. But not only is it a mark of limitation to refuse all interest to such a work as, for example, M. Cabanel's "Birth of Venus," in the painting of which a vast deal of technical expertness is enjoyably evident, and which in every respect of motive and execution is far above similar things done elsewhere than in France; it is a still greater error to confound such painters as M. Cabanel and M. Bouguereau with other painters whose classic temperament has been subjected to the universal romantic influence equally with theirs, but whose production is as different from theirs as is that of the thorough and pure romanticists, the truly poetic painters.

The instinct of simplification is an intelligent and sound one. Its satisfaction is a necessary preliminary to efficient action of any kind, and indeed the basis of all fruitful philosophy. But in criticism this instinct can only be satisfied intelligently and soundly by a consideration of everything appealing to consideration, and not at all by heated and wilful, or superior and supercilious, exclusions. Catholicity of appreciation is the secret of critical felicity. To follow the line of least resistance, not to take into account those elements of a problem, those characteristics of a subject, to which, superficially and at first thought, one is insensitive, is to dispense one's self from a great deal of particularly disagreeable industry, but the result is only transitorily agreeable to the sincere intelligence. It is in criticism, I think, though no doubt in criticism alone, preferable to lose one's self in a maze of perplexity--distressing as this is to the critic who appreciates the indispensability of clairvoyance in criticism--rather than to reach swiftly and simply a conclusion which candor would have foreseen as the inevitable and unjudicial result of following one's own likes and whims, and one's contentment with which must be alloyed with a haunting sense of insecurity. In criticism it is perhaps better to keep balancing counter-considerations than to determine brutally by excluding a whole set of them because of the difficulty of assigning them their true weight. In this way, at least, one preserves the attitude of poise, and poise is perhaps the one essential element of criticism. In a word, that catholicity of sensitiveness which may be called mere impressionism, behind which there is no body of doctrine at all, is more truly critical than intolerant depreciation or unreflecting enthusiasm. "The main thing to do," says Mr. Arnold, in a significant passage, "is to get one's self out of the way and let humanity judge."

It is temptingly simple to deny all importance to painters who are not poetic painters. And the temptation is especially seductive when the prosaic painters are paralleled by such a distinguished succession of their truly poetic brethren as are the painters of the romantic epoch who are possessed of the classic temperament. But real criticism immediately suggests that prose has its place in painting as in literature. In literature we do not insist even that the poets be poetic. Poetic is not the epithet that would be applied, for instance, to French classic verse or the English verse of the eighteenth century, compared with the poetry, French or English, which we mean when we speak of poetry. Yet no one would think of denying the value of Dryden or even of Boileau. No one would even insist that, distinctly prosaic as are the qualities of Boileau--and I should say his was a crucial instance--he would have done better to abjure verse. And painting, in a wide sense, is just as legitimately the expression of ideas in form and color as literature is the expression of ideas in words. It is perfectly plain that Meissonier was not especially enamoured of beauty, as Corot, as Troyon, as Decamps was. But nothing could be less critical than to deny Meissouier's importance and the legitimate interest he has for every educated and intelligent person, in spite of his literalness and his insensitiveness to the element of beauty, and indeed to any truly pictorial significance whatever in the wide range of subjects that he essayed, with, in an honorable sense, such distinguished success.

Especially in America, I think, where of recent years we have shown an Athenian sensitiveness to new impressions, the direct descendants of the classic period of French painting have suffered from the popularity of the Fontainebleau group. Their legitimate attachment to art, instead of the Fontainebleau absorption in nature, has given them a false reputation of artificiality. But the prose element in art has its justification as well as the poetic, and it is witness of a narrow culture to fail in appreciation of its admirable accomplishment. The academic wing of the French romantic painting is marked precisely by a breadth of culture that is itself a source of agreeable and elevated interest. The neo-Grec painters are thoroughly educated. They lack the picturesque and unexpected note of their poetic brethren--they lack the moving and interpreting, the elevating and exquisite touch of these; nay, they lack the penetrating distinction that radiates even from rusticity itself when it is inspired and transfigured as it appears in such works as those of Millet and Rousseau. But their distinction is not less real for being the distinction of cultivation rather than altogether native and absolute. It is perhaps even more marked, more pervasive, more directly associated with the painter's aim and effect. One feels that they are familiar with the philosophy of art, its history and practice, that they are articulate and eclectic, that for being less personal and powerful their horizon is less limited, their purely intellectual range, at all events, and in many cases their aesthetic interest, wider. They have more the cultivated man's bent for experimentation, for variety. They care more scrupulously for perfection, for form. With a far inferior sense of reality and far less felicity in dealing with it, their sapient skill in dealing with the abstractions of art is more salient. To be blind to their successful handling of line and mass and movement, is to neglect a source of refined pleasure. To lament their lack of poetry is to miss their admirable rhetoric; to regret their imperfect feeling for decorativeness is to miss their delightful decorum.

V

As one has, however, so often occasion to note in France--where in every field of intellectual effort the influence of schools and groups and movements is so great that almost every individuality, no matter how strenuous, falls naturally and intimately into association with some one of them--there is every now and then an exception that escapes these categories and stands quite by itself. In modern painting such exceptions, and widely different from each other as the poles, are Couture and Puvis de Chavannes. Better than in either the true romanticists with the classic strain, or the academic romanticists with the classic temperament, the blending of the classic and romantic inspirations is illustrated in Couture. The two are in him, indeed, actually fused. In Puvis de Chavannes they appear in a wholly novel combination; his classicism is absolutely unacademic, his romanticism unreal beyond the verge of mysticism, and so preoccupied with visions that he may almost be called a man for whom the actual world does *not* exist--in the converse of Gautier's phrase. His distinction is wholly personal. He lives evidently on an exceedingly high plane--dwells habitually in the delectable uplands of the intellect. The fact that his work is almost wholly decorative is not at all accidental. His talent, his genius if one chooses, requires large spaces, vast dimensions. There has been a great deal of rather profitless discussion as to whether he expressly imitates the *primitifs* or reproduces them sympathetically. But really he does neither; he deals with their subjects occasionally, but always in a completely modern, as well as a thoroughly personal, way. His color is as original as his general treatment and composition. He had no schooling, in the Ecole des Beaux Arts sense. A brief period in Henri Scheffer's studio, three months under Couture, after he had begun life in an altogether different field of effort, yielded him all the explicit instruction he ever had. His real study was done in Italy, in the presence of the old masters of Florence. With this equipment he revolutionized modern decoration, established, at any rate, a new convention for it. His convention is a little definite, a little bald. One may discuss it apart from his own handling of it, even. It is a shade too express, too confident, too little careless both of tradition and of the typical qualities that secure permanence. In other hands one can easily imagine how insipid it might become. It has too little body, its scheme is too timorous, too vaporous to be handled by another. Puvis de Chavannes will probably have few successful imitators. But one must immediately add that if he does not found a school, his own work is, perhaps for that reason, at all events in spite of it, among the most important of the day. Quite unperturbed by current discussions, which are certainly of the noisiest by which the current of artistic development was ever deflected, he has kept on his way, and has finally won all suffrages for an aesthetic expression that is really antagonistic to the general aesthetic spirit of his time.

Puvis de Chavannes is, perhaps, the most interesting figure in French painting to-day. Couture is little more than a name. It is curious to consider why. Twenty years ago he was still an important figure. He had been an unusually successful teacher. Many American painters of distinction, especially, were at one time his pupils--Hunt, La Farge, George Butler. He theorized as much, as well--perhaps even better than--he painted. His "Entretiens d'atelier" are as good in their way as his "Baptism of the Prince Imperial." He had a very distinguished talent, but he was too distinctly clever--clever to the point of sophistication. In this respect he was distinctly a man of the nineteenth century. His great work, "Romains de la Decadence," created as fine an effect at the Centenary Exhibition of the Paris World's Fair in 1889 as it does in the Louvre, whence it was then transferred, but it was distinctly a decorative effect--the effect of a fine panel in the general mass of color and design; it made a fine centre. It remains his greatest performance, the performance upon which chiefly his fame will depend, though as painting it lacks the quality and breadth of "Le Fauconnier," perhaps the most interesting of his works to painters themselves, and of the "Day-Dreams" of the New York Metropolitan Museum of Art. Its permanent interest perhaps will be the historical one, due to the definiteness with which it assigns Couture his position in the evolution of French painting. It shows, as everything of Couture shows, the absence of any pictorial feeling so profound and personal as to make an impression strong enough to endure indefinitely. And it has not, on the other hand, the interest of reality--that faithful and enthusiastic rendering of the external world which gives importance to and fixes the character of the French painting of the present day.

Had Regnault lived, he would have more adequately--or should I say more plausibly?--marked the transition from romanticism to realism. Temperamentally he was clearly a thorough romanticist--far more so, for instance, than his friend Fortuny, whose intellectual reserve is always conspicuous. He essayed the most vehement kind of subjects, even in the classical field, where he treated them with truly romantic truculence. He was himself always, moreover, and ideally cared as little for nature as a fairy-story teller. In this sense he was more romantic than the romanticists. His "Automedon," his portrait of General Prim, even his "Salome," are wilful in a degree that is either superb or superficial, as one looks at them; but at any rate they are romantic *a outrance*. At the same time it was unmistakably the aspect of things rather than their significance, rather than his view of them, that appealed to him. He was farther away from the classic inspiration than any other romanticist of his fellows; and at the same time he cared for the external world more on its own account and less for its suggestions, than any painter of equal force before Courbet and Bastien-Lepage. The very fact that he was not, intellectually speaking, wholly *dans son assiette*, as the French say, shows that he was a genius of a transitional moment. One's final thought of him is that he died young, and one thinks so not so much because of the dramatic tragedy of his taking off by possibly the last Prussian bullet fired in the war of 1870-71, as because of the essentially experimental character of his painting. Undoubtedly he would have done great things. And undoubtedly they would have been different from those that he did; probably in the direction--already indicated in his most dignified performance--of giving more consistency, more vivid definiteness, more reality, even, to his already striking conceptions.

III

REALISTIC PAINTING
I

To an intelligence fully and acutely alive, its own time must, I think, be more interesting than any other. The sentimental, the scholastic, the speculative temperament may look before or after with longing or regret; but that sanity of mind which is practical and productive must find its most agreeable sensations in the data to which it is intimately and inexorably related. The light upon Greek literature and art for which we study Greek history, the light upon Roman history for which we study Latin literature and art, are admirable to us in very exact proportion as we study them for our ends. To every man and every nation that really breathes, true vitality of soul depends upon saying to one's self, with an emotion of equivalent intensity to the emotion of patriotism celebrated in Scott's familiar lines, This is my own, my native era and environment. Culture is impossible apart from cosmopolitanism, but self-respect is more indispensable even than culture. French art alone at the present time possesses absolute self-respect. It possesses this quality in an eminent, in even an excessive degree; but it possesses it, and in virtue of it is endued with a preservative quality that saves it from the emptiness of imitation and the enervation of dilettantism. It has, in consequence, escaped that recrudescence of the primitive and inchoate known in England and among ourselves as pre-Raphaelitism. It has escaped also that almost abject worship of classic models which Winckelmann and Canova made universal in Germany and Italy--not to speak of its echoes elsewhere. It has always stood on its own feet, and, however lacking in the higher qualities of imaginative initiative, on the one hand,

and however addicted to the academic and the traditional on the other, has always both respected its aesthetic heritage and contributed something of its own thereto.

Why should not one feel the same quick interest, the same instinctive pride in his time as in his country? Is not sympathy with what is modern, instant, actual, and apposite a fair parallel of patriotism? Neglect of other times in the "heir of all the ages" is analogous to chauvinism, and indicative of as ill-judged an attitude as that of provincial blindness to other contemporary points of view and systems of philosophy than one's own. Culture is equally hostile to both, and in art culture is as important a factor as it is in less special fields of activity and endeavor. But in art, as elsewhere, culture is a means to an actual, present end, and the pre-Raphaelite sentiment that dictates mere reproduction of what was once a genuine expression is as sterile as servile imitation of exotic modes of thought, dress, and demeanor is universally felt to be. The past--the antique, the renaissance, the classic, and romantic ideals are to be used, not adopted; in the spirit of Goethe, at once the most original of modern men and the most saturated with culture, exhibited in his famous saying: "Nothing do I call my own which having inherited I have not reconquered for myself."

It would indeed be a singular thing were the field of aesthetics the only one uninvaded by the scientific spirit of the time. The one force especially characteristic of our era is, I suppose, the scientific spirit. It is at any rate everywhere manifest, and it possesses the best intellects of the century. *A priori* one may argue about its hostility, essential or other, to the artistic, the constructive spirit; but to do so is at the most to beat the air, to waste one's breath, to Ruskinize, in a word. Interest in life and the world, instead of speculation or self-expression, is the "note" of the day. The individual has withered terribly. He is supplanted by the type. Materialism has its positive gospel; it is not at all the formulated expression of Goethe's "spirit that denies." Nature has acquired new dignity. She cannot be studied too closely, nor too long. The secret of the universe is now pursued through observation, as formerly it was through fasting and prayer. Nothing is sacred nowadays because everything receives respect. If absolute beauty is now smiled at as a chimera, it is because beauty is perceived everywhere. Whatever is may not be right--the maxim has too much of an *ex cathedra* sound--but whatever is is interesting. Our attitude is at once humbler and more curious. The sense of the immensity, the immeasurableness of things, is more intimate and profound. What one may do is more modestly conceived; what might be done, more justly appreciated. There is less confidence and more aspiration. The artist's eye is "on the object" in more concentrated gaze than ever heretofore. If his sentiment, his poetry, is no longer "inevitable," as Wordsworth complained Goethe's was not, it is more reverent, at any rate more circumspect. If he is less exalted he is more receptive--he is more alive to impressions for being less of a philosopher. If he scouts authority, if even he accepts somewhat weakly the thraldom of dissent from traditional standards and canons, it is because he is convinced that the material with which he has to deal is superior to all canons and standards. If he esteems truth more than beauty, it is because what he thinks truth is more beautiful in his eyes than the stereotyped beauty he is adjured to attain. In any case, the distinction of the realistic painters--like that of the realists in literature, where, also, it need not be said, France has been in the lead--is measurably to have got rid of solecisms; to have made, indeed, obvious solecisms, and solecisms of conception as well as of execution, a little ridiculous. It is, to be sure, equally ridiculous to subject romantic productions to realistic standards, to blind one's self to the sentiment that saturates such romantic works as Scott's and Dumas's, or Gericault's and Diaz's, and is wholly apposite to its own time and point of view. The great difficulty with a principle is that it is universal, and that when we deal with facts of any kind whatever, universality is an impossible ideal. Scott and Gericault are, nowadays, in what we have come to deem essentials, distinctly old-fashioned. It might be well to try and imitate them, if imitation had any salt in it, which it has not; or if it were possible to do what they did with their different inspiration, which it is not. Mr. Stevenson is, I think, an example of the danger of essaying this latter in literature, just as a dozen eminent painters of less talent--for no one has so much talent as Mr. Stevenson--are examples in painting. But there are a thousand things, not only in the technic of the romanticists but in their whole attitude toward their art and their material, that are nowadays impossible to sincere and spontaneous artists. Details which have no importance whatever in the ***ensemble*** of the romantic artist are essential to the realist. Art does not stand still. Its canons change. There is a constant evolution in its standards, its requirements. A conventional background is no more an error in French classic painting than in tapestry; a perfunctory scheme of pure chiaro-oscuro is no blemish in one of Diaz's splendid forest landscapes; such phenomena in a work of Raffaelli or Pointelin would jar, because, measured by the standards to which modern men must, through the very force of evolution itself, subscribe, they can but appear solecisms. In a different set of circumstances, under a different inspiration, and with a different artistic attitude, solecisms they certainly are not. But, as Thackeray makes Ethel Newcome say, "We belong to our belongings." Our circumstances, inspiration, artistic attitude, are involuntary and possess us as our other belongings do.

In Gautier's saying, for instance, "I am a man for whom the visible world exists," which I have quoted as expressing the key-note of the romantic epoch, it is to be noted that the visible world is taken as a spectacle simply--significant, suggestive or merely stimulant, in accordance with individual bent. Gautier and the romanticists generally had little concern for its structure. To many of them it was indeed rather a canvas than a spectacle even--just as to many, if not to most, of the realists it is its structure rather than its significance that altogether appeals; the romanticists in general sketched their ideas and impressions upon it, as the naturalists have in the main studied its aspects and constitution, careless of the import of these, pictorially or otherwise. Indeed one is tempted often to inquire of the latter, Why so much interest in what apparently seems to you of so little import? Are we never to have your skill, your observation, your amassing of "documents" turned to any account? Where is the realistic tragedy, comedy, epic, composition of any sort? Courbet's "Cantonniers," Manet's "Bar," or Bastien-Lepage's "Joan of Arc," perhaps. But what is indisputable is, that we are irretrievably committed to the present general aesthetic attitude and inspiration, and must share not only the romanticists' impatience with academic formulae and conventions, but the realists' devotion to life and the world as they actually exist. The future may be different, but we are living in the present, and what is important is, after all, to live. It is also so difficult that not to take the line of least resistance is fatuity.

II

It is at least an approximation to ascribe the primacy of realism to Courbet, though ascriptions of the kind are at best approximations. Not only was he the first, or among the first, to feel the interest and importance of the actual world as it is and for what it is rather than for what it suggests, but his feeling in this direction is intenser than that of anyone else. Manet was preoccupied with the values of objects and spaces. Bastien-Lepage, while painting these with the most scrupulous fidelity, was nevertheless always attentive to the significance and import of what he painted. Courbet was a pure pantheist. He was possessed by the material, the physical, the actual. He never varies it a hair's-breadth. He never lifts it a fraction of a degree. But by his very absorption in it he dignifies it immensely. He illustrates magnificently its possibilities. He brings out into the plainest possible view its inherent, integral, aesthetic quality, independent of any extraneity. No painter ever succeeded so well with so little art, one is tempted to say. Beside his, the love of nature which we ascribe to the ordinary realist is a superficial emotion. He had the ***sentiment*** of reality in the highest degree; he had it intensely. If he did not represent nature with the searching subtlety of later painters, he is certainly the forerunner of naturalism. He has absolutely no ideality. He is blind to all intimations of immortality, all unearthly voices.

Yet it would be wholly an error to suppose him a mere literalist. No one is farther removed from the painstaking, grubbing imitators of detail so justly denounced and ridiculed by Mr. Whistler. He has the generalizing faculty in very distinguished degree, and in very large measure. Every trait of his talent, indeed, is large, manly; but for a certain qualification--which must be made--one might add, Olympian. This qualification perhaps may be not unfairly described as earthiness--never an agreeable trait, and one to which probably is due the depreciation of Courbet that is so popular even among appreciative critics. It is easy to characterize Courbet as brutal and material, but what is easy is generally not exact. What one glibly stigmatizes as brutality and grossness may, after all, be something of a particularly strong savor, enjoyed by the painter himself with a gusto too sterling and instinctive to be justifiably neglected, much less contemned. The first thing to do in estimating an artist's accomplishment, which is to place one's self at his point of view, is, in Courbet's case, unusually difficult. We are all dreamers, more or less--in more or less desultory fashion--and can all appreciate that prismatic turn of what is real and actual into a position wherein it catches glints of the imagination. The imagination is a universal touchstone. The sense of reality is a special, an individual faculty. When one is poetizing in an amateur, a dilettante way, as most of us poetize, a picture of Courbet, which seems to flaunt and challenge the imagination in virtue of its defiant reality, its insistence on the value and significance of the prosaic and the actual, appears coarse and crude. It is not, however. It is very far from that. It is rather elemental than elementary--in itself a prodigious distinction. No modern painter has felt more intensely and reproduced more vigorously the sap that runs through and vivifies the various forms of natural phenomena. To censure his shortcomings, to regret his imaginative incompleteness, is to miss him altogether.

It is easy to say he had all the coarseness without the sentiment of the French peasantry, whence he sprang; that his political radicalism attests a lack of the serenity of spirit indispensable to the sincere artist; that he had no conception of the beautiful, the exquisite--the fact remains that he triumphs over all his deficiencies, and in very splendid fashion. He is, in truth, of all the realists for whom he discovered the way, and set the pace, as it were, one of the two naturalistic painters who have shown in any high degree the supreme artistic faculty--that of generalization. However impressive Manet's picture may be; however brilliant Monet's endeavor to reproduce sunlight may seem; however refined and elegant Degas's delicate selection of pictorial material--for broad and masterful generalization, for enduing what he painted with an interest deeper than its surface and underlying its aspect, Courbet has but one rival among realistic painters. I mean, of course, Bastien-Lepage.

There is an important difference between the two. In Courbet the sentiment of reality dominates the realism of the technic; in Bastien-Lepage the technic is realistically carried infinitely farther, but the sentiment quite transcends realism. Imagine Courbet essaying a "Jeanne d'Arc!" Bastien-Lepage painting Courbet's "Cantonniers" would not have stopped, as Courbet has done, with expressing their vitality, their actual interest, but at the same time that he represented them in far greater technical completeness he would also have occupied himself with their psychology. He is indeed quite as distinctly a psychologist as he is a painter. His favorite problem, aside from that of technical perfection, which perhaps equally haunted him, is the rendering of that resigned, bewildered, semi-hypnotic, vaguely and yet intensely longing spiritual expression to be noted by those who have the eyes to see it in the faces and attitudes now of the peasant laborer, now of the city pariah. All

his peasant women are potentially Jeannes d'Arc--"Les Foins," "Tired," "Petite Fau-
vette," for example. The "note" is still more evident in the "London Bootblack" and
the "London Flower-girl," in which the outcast "East End" spiritlessness of the British capital is caught and fixed with a Zola-like veracity and vigor. Such a phase as
this is not so much pictorial or poetic, as psychological. Bastien-Lepage's happiness
in rendering it is a proof of the exceeding quickness and sureness of his observation;
but his preoccupation with it is equally strong proof of his interest in the things of
the mind as well as in those of the senses. This is his great distinction, I think. He
beats the realist on his own ground (except perhaps Monet and his followers--I remember no attempt of his to paint sunlight), but he is imaginative as well. He is not,
on the other hand, to be in anywise associated with the romanticists. Degas's acid
characterization of him, as "the Bouguereau of the modern movement," is only just,
if we remember what very radical and fundamental changes the "modern movement" implies in general attitude as well as in special expression. I should be inclined, rather, to apply the analogy to M. Dagnan-Bouveret, though here, too, with
many reserves looking mainly to the difference between true and vapid sentiment.

It is interesting to note, however, the almost exclusively intellectual character of this imaginative side of Bastien-Lepage. He does not view his material with
any apparent sympathy, such as one notes, or at all events divines, in Millet. Both
were French peasants; but whereas Millet's interest in his fellows is instinctive and
absorbing, Bastien-Lepage's is curious and detached. If his pictures ever succeed in
moving us, it is impersonally, in virtue of the camera-like scrutiny he brings to bear
on his subject, and the effectiveness with which he renders it, and of the reflections
which we institute of ourselves, and which he fails to stimulate by even the faintest
trace of a loving touch or the betrayal of any sympathetic losing of himself in his
theme. You feel just the least intimation of the ***doctrinaire***, the systematic aloof-
ness of the spectator. In moral attitude as well as in technical expression he no more
assimilates the various phases of his material, to reproduce them afterward in new
and original combination, than he expresses the essence of landscape in general, as
the Fontainebleau painters do even in their most photographic moments. Both his
figures and his landscapes are clearly portraits--typical and not merely individual,
to be sure, but somehow not exactly creations. His skies are the least successful portions of his pictures, I think; one must generalize easily to make skies effective, and

perhaps it is not fanciful to note the frequency of high horizons in his work.

The fact remains that Bastien-Lepage stands at the head of the modern move-ment in many ways. His friend, M. Andre Theuriet, has shown, in a brochure pub-lished some years ago, that he was himself as interesting as his pictures. He took his art very seriously, and spoke of it with a dignity rather uncommon in the atmo-sphere of the studios, where there is apt to be more enthusiasm than reflection. I recall vividly the impatience with which he once spoke to me of painting "to show what you can do." His own standard was always the particular ideal he had formed, never within the reach of his ascertained powers. And whatever he did, one may say, illustrates the sincerity and elevation of this remark, whether one's mood in-cline one to care most for this psychological side--undoubtedly the more nearly unique side--of his work, or for such exquisite things as his "Forge" or the portrait of Mme Sarah Bernhardt. Incontestably he has the true tradition, and stands in the line of the great painters. And he owes his permanent place among them not less to his perception that painting has a moral and significant, as well as a representative and decorative sanction, than to his perfect harmony with his own time in his way of illustrating this--to his happy fusion of aspect admirably rendered with profound and stimulating suggestion.

III

Of the realistic landscape painters, the strict impressionists apart, none is more eminent than M. Cazin, whose work is full of interest, and if at times it leaves one a little cold, this is perhaps an affair of the beholder's temperament rather than of M. Cazin's. He is a thoroughly original painter, and, what is more at the present day, an imaginative one. He sees in his own way the nature that we all see, and paints it not literally but personally. But his landscapes invariably attest, above all, an attentive study of the phenomena of light and air, and their truthfulness is the more marked for the personality they illustrate. The impression they make is of a very clairvoy-ant and enthusiastic observation exercised by an artist who takes more pleasure in appreciation than in expression, whose pleasure in his expression is subordinate to his interest in the external world, and in large measure confined to the delight every artist has in technical felicity when he can attain it. Their skies are beautifully observed--graduated in value with delicate verisimilitude from the horizon up, and wind-swept, or drenched with mist, or ringing clear, as the motive may dictate. All objects take their places with a precision that, nevertheless, is in nowise pedantic, and is perfectly free. Cazin's palette is, moreover, a thoroughly individual one. It is very pure, and if its range is not great, it is at any rate not grayed into insipidity and ineffectualness, but is as positive as if it were more vivid. A distinct air of elegance, a true sense of style, is noteworthy in many of his pictures; not only in the important ones, but occasionally when the theme is so slight as to need hardly any composition whatever--the mere placing of a tree, its outline, its relation to a bank or a roadway, are often unmistakably distinguished. Cazin is not exclusively a landscape painter, and though the landscape element in all his works is a dominant one, even in his "Hagar and Ishmael in the Desert," and his "Judith Setting out for Holofernes's Camp" (in which latter one can hardly identify the heroine at all), the fact that he is not a landscape painter, pure and simple, like Harpignies and Pointelin, perhaps accounts for his inferiority to them in landscape sentiment. In France it is generally assumed that to devote one's self exclusively to any one branch of painting is to betray limitations, and there are few painters who would not resent being called landscapists. Something, perhaps, is lost in this way. It witnesses a greater pride in accomplishment than in instinctive bent. But however that may be, Cazin never penetrates to the sentiment of nature that one feels in such a work as Harpignies's "Moonrise," for example, or in almost any of Pointelin's grave and impressive landscapes. Hardly less truthful, I should say, though perhaps less intimately and elaborately real (a romanticist would say less superficially real) than Cazin's, the work of both these painters is more pictorial. They have a quicker sense for the beautiful, I think. They feel very certainly much more deeply the suggestiveness of a scene. They are not so *debonnaires* in the presence of their problems. In a sense, for that reason, they understand them better. There is very little feeling of the desert, the illimitable space, where, according to Balzac, God is and man is not, in the "Hagar and Ishmael;" indeed there seems to have been no attempt on the part of the painter to express any. True as his sand-heap is, you feel somehow that there may be a kitchen-garden or the entrance to a coal-mine on the other side of it, or a little farther along. And the landscape of the "Judith," fine as its sweep is, and admirable as are the cool tone and clear distance of the picture, might really be that of the "south meadow" of some particular "farm" or other.

The contrast which Guillaumet presents to Fromentin affords a very striking illustration of the growth of the realistic spirit in recent years. Fromentin is so admirable a painter that I can hardly fancy any appreciative person wishing him different. His devoted admirer and biographer, M. Louis Gonse, admits, and indeed expressly records, Fromentin's own lament over the insufficiency of his studies. Fond as he was of horses, for instance, he does not know them as a draughtsman with the science of such a conventional painter in many other respects as Schreyer. But it is not in the slightly amateurish nature of his technical equipment--realized perfectly by himself, of course, as the first critic of the technic of painting among all who have ventured upon the subject--that his painting differs from Guillaumet's. It is his whole point of view. His Africa is that of the critic, the *litterateur*, the *raffine*. Guillaumet's is Africa itself. You feel before Guillaumet's Luxembourg canvases, as in looking over the slightest of his vivid memoranda, that you are getting in an acute and concentrated form the sensations which the actual scenes and types rendered by the painter would stimulate in you, supposing, of course, that you were sufficiently sensitive. Fromentin, in comparison, is occupied in picture-making--giving you a beautifully colored and highly intelligent pictorial report as against Guillaumet's actual reproduction. There is no question as to which of the two painters has the greater personal interest; but it is just as certain that for abiding value and enduring charm personal interest must either be extremely great or else yield to the interest inherent in the material dealt with, an interest that Guillaumet brings out with a felicity and a puissance that are wholly extraordinary, and that nowadays meet with a readier and more sympathetic recognition that even such delicate personal charm as that of Fromentin.

IV

So thoroughly has the spirit of realism fastened upon the artistic effort of the present that temperaments least inclined toward interest in the actual feel its influences, and show the effects of these. The most recalcitrant illustrate this tech-

nically, however rigorously they may preserve their point of view. They paint at
least more circumspectly, however they may think and feel. An historical painter
like Jean Paul Laurens, interested as he is in the memorable moments and dramatic
incidents of the past, and exhibiting as he does, first of all, a sense of what is ideally
forceful and heroic, is nevertheless clearly concerned for the realistic value of his
representation far more than a generation ago he would have been. When Luminais
paints a scene from Gaulish legend, he is not quite, but nearly, as careful to make it
pictorially real as he is to have it dramatically effective. M. Francois Flameng, ex-
panding his book illustration into a mammoth canvas commemorative of the Ven-
dean insurrection, is almost daintily fastidious about the naturalistic aspect of his
abundant detail. M. Benjamin-Constant's artificially conceived seraglio scenes are
as realistically rendered as is indicated by a recent caricature depicting an aston-
ished sneak-thief, foiled in an attempted rape of the jewels in a sultana's diadem,
painted with such deceptive illusoriness by M. Benjamin-Constant's clever brush.
The military painters, Detaille, De Neuville, Berne-Bellecour, do not differ from
Vernet more by painting incidents instead of phases of warfare, by substituting the
touch of dramatic *genre* for epic conceptions, than they do by the scrupulously
naturalistic rendering that in them supplants the old academic symbolism. Their
dragoons and *fantassins* are not merely more real in what they do, but in how
they look. Vernet's look like tin soldiers by comparison; certainly like soldiers *de
convenance*. Aime Morot evidently used instantaneous photography, and his magnificent cavalry charges suggest not only carnage, but Muybridge as well.

   The great portrait-painters of the day--Carolus-Duran, Bonnat, Ribot--are realists to the core. They are very far from being purely portrait-painters of course,
and their realism shows itself with splendid distinction in other works. Few painters of the nude have anything to their credit as fine as the figure M. Carolus-Duran
exhibited at the Paris Exposition in 1889. Ribot's "Saint Sebastian" is one of the most
powerful pictures of modern French art. Bonnat's "Christ" became at once famous.
Each picture is painted with a vigor and point of realistic detail that are peculiar
to our own time; painted to-day, Bonnat's fine and sculptural "Fellah Woman and
Child," of the Metropolitan Museum, would be accented in a dozen ways in which
now it is not. But it is perhaps in portraiture that the eminence of these painters is
most explicit. They are at the head of contemporary portraitists, at all events. And

their portraits are almost defiantly real, void often of arrangement, and as little artificial as the very frequently prosaic atmosphere appertaining to their sometimes
very stark subjects suggests. A portrait by Bonnat blinks nothing in the subject; its
aim and accomplishment are the rendering of the character in a vivid fashion--in-
cluding the reproduction of cobalt cravats and creased trousers even--which would
have mightily embarrassed Van Dyck or Velasquez. Ribot reproduces Ribera often,
but he deals with fewer externals, fewer effects, taken in the widest sense. Carolus-
Duran, the "swell" portrait-painter of the day, artificial as he may be in the quality
of his mind, nevertheless seeks and attains, first of all, the sense of an even exaggerated life-likeness in his charming sitters. They are, first of all, people; the pictorial element takes care of itself; sometimes even--so overmastering is the realistic
tendency--the plush of the chair, the silk of the robe, the cut of the coat, seems, to
an observer who thinks of the old traditions of Titian, of Raphael, of Moroni, unduly emphasized, even for realism.

V

One element of modernity is a certain order of eclecticism. It is not the eclecticism of the Bolognese painters, for example, illustrating the really hopeless attempt
to combine the supposed and superficial excellences, always dissociated from the
essence, of different points of view. It is a free choice of attitude, rather, due to the
release of the individual from the thraldom of conformity that ruled even during the
romantic epoch. Hence a great deal of admirable work, of which one hardly thinks
whether it is realistic or not, side by side with the more emphatic expressions of the
realistic spirit. And this work is of all degrees of realism, never, however, getting
very far away from the naturalistic basis on which more and more everyone is coming to insist as the necessary and only solid pedestal of any flight of fancy. Baudry
is perhaps the nearest of the really great men to the Bolognese order of eclecticism. I suppose he must be classed among the really great men, so many painters
of intelligence place him there, though I must myself plead the laic privilege of a
slight scepticism as to whether time will approve their enthusiasm. He is certainly
very effective, and in certainly his own way, idle as it is to say that his drafts on the

great Italians are no greater than those of Raphael on the antique frescos. He had a great love of color and a native instinct for it; with perhaps more appreciation than invention, his imagination has something very personal in the zealous enthusiasm with which he exercised it, though I think it must be admitted that his reflections of Tiepolo, Titian, Tintoretto and his attenuated expansions of Michael Angelo's condensed grandiosity, recall the eclecticism of the Carracci far more than that of Raphael. But his manner is the modern manner, and it is altogether more effective, more "fetching," to use a modern term, than anything purely academic can be. Elie Delaunay, another master of decoration, is, on the other hand, as real as the most rigorous literalist could ask of a painter of decorative works. Chartran, who has an individual charm that both Baudry and Delaunay lack, inferior as he is to them in sweep and power, is perhaps in this respect midway between the two. Clairin is, like Mazerolles, a pure *fantaisiste*. Dubufe *fils*, whose at least equally famous father ranks in a somewhat similar category with Couture, shows a distinct advance upon him in reality of rendering, as the term would be understood at present.

In other departments of painting the note of realism is naturally still more universally apparent; but as in the work of the painters of decoration it is often most noticeable as an undertone, indicating a point of departure rather than an aim. Bonvin is a realist only as Chardin, as Van der Meer of Delft, as Nicholas Maes were, before the jargon of realism had been thought of. He is, first of all, an exquisite artist, in love with the beautiful in reality, finding in it the humblest material, and expressing it with the gentlest, sweetest, aesthetic severity and composure imaginable. The most fastidious critic needs but a touch of human feeling to convert any characterization of this most refined and elevated of painters into pure panegyric. Vollon's touch is felicity itself, and it is evident that he takes more pleasure in exercising and exploiting it than in its successful imitation, striking as its imitative quality is. Gervex and Duez are very much more than impressionists, both in theory and practice. There is nothing polemic in either. Painters extol in the heartiest way the color, the creative coloration of Gervex's "Rolla," quite aside from its dramatic force or its truth of aspect. Personal feeling is clearly the inspiration of every work of Duez, not the demonstration of a theory of treating light and atmosphere. The same may be said of Roll at his best, as in his superb rendering of what may be called the modern painter's conception of the myth of Europa. Compared with Paul Veronese's admirable classic, that violates all the unities (which Veronese, neverthe-less, may readily be pardoned by all but literalists and theorists for neglecting), this splendid nude girl in ***plein air***, flecked with splotches of sunlight filtered through a sieve of leafage, with her realistic taurine companion, and their environment of veridically rendered out-of-doors, may stand for an illustrative definition of moder-nity; but what you feel most of all is Roll. It is ten chances to one that he has never even been to Venice or thought of Veronese. He has not always been so successful; as when in his "Work" he earned Degas's acute comment: "A crowd is made with five persons, not with fifty." ("Il y a cinquante figures, mais je ne vois pas la foule; on fait une foule avec cinq, et non pas avec cinquante.") But he has always been someone. Compare with him L'Hermitte, a painter who illustrates sometimes the possibility of being an artificial realist. His "Vintage" at the Metropolitan Museum, his "Harvesters" at the Luxembourg, are excellently real and true in detail, but in idea and general expression they might compete for the prix de Rome. The same is measurably true of Lerolle, whose pictures are more sympathetic--sometimes they are ***very*** sympathetic--but on the whole display less power. But in each instance the advocate ***a outrance*** of realism may justly, I think, maintain that a painter with a natural predisposition toward the insipidity of the academic has been saved from it by the inherent sanity and robustness of the realistic method. Jean Beraud, even, owes something to the way in which his verisimilitude of method has reinforced his artistic powers. His delightful Parisiennes--modistes' messengers crossing wet glistening pavements against a background of gray mist accented with poster-bedi-zened kiosks and regularly recurring horse-chestnut trees; ***elegantes*** at prayer, in somewhat distracted mood, on ***prie-dieus*** in the vacant and vapid Paris churches; seated at cafe tables on the busy, leisurely boulevards, or posing ***tout bonnement*** for the reproduction of the most fascinating feminine ***ensemble*** in the world--owe their charm (I may say again their "fetchingness") to the faithfulness with which their portraitist has studied, and the fidelity with which he has reproduced, their differing types, more than to any personal expression of his own view of them. Fancy Beraud's masterpiece, the Salle Graffard--that admirable characterization of crankdom embodied in a socialist reunion--painted by an academic painter. How absolutely it would lose its pith, its force, its significance, even its true distinction. And his "Magdalen at the Pharisee's House," which is almost equally impressive--

far more impressive of course in a literary and, I think, legitimate, sense--owes even its literary effectiveness to its significant realism.

What the illustrators of the present day owe to the naturalistic method, it is almost superfluous to point out. "Illustrators" in France are, in general, painters as well, some of them very eminent painters. Daumier, who passed in general for a contributor to illustrated journals, even such journals as *Le Petit Journal pour Rire*, was not only a genius of the first rank, but a painter of the first class. Monvel and Montenard at present are masterly painters. But in their illustration as well as in their painting, they show a notable change from the illustration of the days of Daumier and Dore. The difference between the elegant (or perhaps rather the handsome) drawings of Bida, an artist of the utmost distinction, and that of the illustrators of the present day who are comparable with him--their name is not legion--is a special attestation of the influence of the realistic ideal in a sphere wherein, if anywhere, one may say, realism reigns legitimately, but wherein also the conventional is especially to be expected. One cannot indeed be quite sure that the temptations of the conventional are resisted by the ultra-realistic illustrators of our own time, Rossi, Beaumont, Albert Lynch, Myrbach. They have certainly a very handy way of expressing themselves; one would be justified in suspecting the labor-saving, the art-sparing kodak, behind many of their most unimpeachable successes. But the attitude taken is quite other than it used to be, and the change that has come over French aesthetic activity in general can be noted in very sharp definition by comparing a book illustrated twenty years ago by Albert Lynch, with, for example, Maupassant's "Pierre et Jean," the distinguished realism of whose text is adequately paralleled--and the implied eulogy is by no means trivial--by the pictorical commentary, so to speak, which this first of modern illustrators has supplied. And an even more striking illustration of the evolution of realistic thought and feeling, as well as of rendering, is furnished by the succession of Forain to Grevin, as an illustrator of the follies of the day, the characteristic traits of the Parisian seamy side, morally speaking. Grevin is as conventional as Murger, in philosophy, and--though infinitely cleverer--as "Mars" in drawing. Forain, with the pencil of a realism truly Japanese, illustrates with sympathetic incisiveness the pitiless pessimism of Flaubert, Goncourt, and Maupassant as well.

VI

But to go back a little and consider the puissant individualities, the great men who have really given its direction to and, as it were, set the pace of, the realistic movement, and for whom, in order more conveniently to consider impressionism pure and simple by itself, I have ventured to disturb the chronological sequence of evolution in French painting--a sequence that, even if one care more for ideas than for chronology, it is more temerarious to vary from in things French than in any others. To go back in a word to Manet; the painter of whom M. Henri Houssaye has remarked: "Manet sowed, M. Bastien-Lepage has reaped."

Manet was certainly one of the most noteworthy painters that France or any other country has produced. His is the great, the very rare, merit of having conceived a new point of view. That he did not illustrate this in its completeness, that he was a sign-post, as Albert Wolff very aptly said, rather an exemplar, is nothing. He was totally unheralded, and he was in his way superb. No one before him had essayed--no one before him had ever thought of--the immense project of breaking, not relatively but absolutely, with the conventional. Looking for the first time at one of his pictures, one says that customary notions, ordinary brushes, traditional processes of even the highest authenticity, have been thrown to the winds. Hence, indeed, the scandal which he caused from the first and which went on increasing, until, owing to the acceptance, with modifications, of his point of view by the most virile and vigorous painters of the day, he became, as he has become, in a sense the head of the corner. Manet's great distinction is to have discovered that the sense of reality is achieved with a thousand-fold greater intensity by getting as near as possible to the *actual*, rather than resting content with the *relative*, value of every detail. Everyone who has painted since Manet has either followed him in this effort or has appeared jejune.

Take as an illustration of the contrary practice such a masterpiece in its way as Gerome's "Eminence Grise." In this picture, skilfully and satisfactorily composed, the relative values of all the colors are admirably, even beautifully, observed. The correspondence of the gamut of values to that of the light and dark scale of such an actual scene is perfect. Before Manet, one could have said that this is all that is required or can be secured, arguing that exact *imitation* of local tints and general tone is impossible, owing to the difference between nature's highest light and lowest dark, and the potentialities of the palette. In other words, one might have said, that inasmuch as you can squeeze absolute white and absolute black out of no tubes, the thing to do is first to determine the scale of your picture and then make every note in it bear the same relation to every other that the corresponding note in nature bears to its fellows in its own corresponding but different scale. This is what Gerome has done in the "Eminence Grise"--a scene, it will be remembered, on a staircase in a palace interior. Manet inquires what would happen to this house of cards shored up into verisimilitude by mere *correspondence*, if Gerome had been asked to cut a window in his staircase and admit the light of out-of-doors into his correspondent but artificial scene. The whole thing would have to be done over again. The scale of the picture running from the highest palette white to the lowest palette dark, and yet the key of an actual interior scene being much nearer middle-tint than the tint of an actual out-of-doors scene, it would be impossible to paint with any verisimilitude the illumination of a window from the outside, the resources of the palette having already been exhausted, every object having been given a local value solely with relation, so far as truth of representation is concerned, to the values of every other object, and no effort being made to get the precise value of the object as it would appear under analogous circumstances in nature.

It may be replied, and I confess I think with excellent reason, that Gerome's picture has no window in it, and therefore that to ask of him to paint a picture as he would if he were painting a different picture, is pedantry. The old masters are still admirable, though they only observed a correspondence to the actual scale of natural values, and were not concerned with imitation of it. But it is to be observed that, successful as their practice is, it is successful in virtue of the unconscious co-operation of the beholder's imagination. And nowadays not only is the exercise of the imagination become for better or worse a little old-fashioned, but the one thing that is insisted on as a starting-point and basis, at the very least, is the sense of reality. And it is impossible to exaggerate the way in which the sense of reality has been intensified by Manet's insistence upon getting as near as possible to the individual values of objects as they are seen in nature--in spite of his abandonment of the practice of painting on a parallel scale. Things now drop into their true place, look as they really do, and count as they count in nature, because the painter is no longer content with giving us change for nature, but tries his best to give us nature itself. Perspective acquires its actual significance, solids have substance and bulk as well as surfaces, distance is perceived as it is in nature, by the actual interposition of atmosphere, chiaro-oscuro is abolished--the ways in which reality is secured being in fact legion the moment real instead of relative values are studied. Something is lost, very likely--an artist cannot be so intensely preoccupied with reality as, since Manet, it has been incumbent on painters to be, without missing a whole range of qualities that are so precious as rightly perhaps to be considered indispensable. Until reality becomes in its turn an effect unconsciously attained, the painter's imagination will be held more or less in abeyance. And perhaps we are justified in thinking that nothing can quite atone for its absence. Meantime, however, it must be acknowledged that Manet first gave us this sense of reality in a measure comparable with that which successively Balzac, Flaubert, Zola gave to the readers of their books--a sense of actuality and vividness beside which the traditionary practice seemed absolutely fanciful and mechanical.

Applying Manet's method, his invention, his discovery, to the painting of out-of-doors, the *plein air* school immediately began to produce landscapes of astonishing reality by confining their effort to those values which it is in the power of pigments to imitate. The possible scale of mere correspondence being of course from one to one hundred, they secured greater truth by painting between twenty and eighty, we may say. Hence the grayness of the most successful French landscapes of the present day--those of Bastien-Lepage's backgrounds, of Cazin's pictures. Sunlight being unpaintable, they confined themselves to the representation of what they could represent. In the interest of truth, of reality, they narrowed the gamut of their modulations, they attempted less, upheld by the certainty of accomplishing more. For a time French landscape was pitched in a minor key. Suddenly Claude Monet appeared. Impressionism, as it is now understood, and as Manet had not succeeded in popularizing it, won instant recognition. Monet's discovery was that light is the most important factor in the painting of out-of-doors. He pushed up the key of landscape painting to the highest power. He attacked the fascinating, but of course demonstrably insolvable, problem of painting sunlight, not illusorily, as Fortuny had done by relying on contrasts of light and dark correspondent in scale, but positively and realistically. He realized as nearly as possible the effect of sunlight--that is to say, he did as well and no better in this respect than Fortuny had done--but he created a much greater illusion of a sunlit landscape than anyone had ever done before him, by painting those parts of his picture not in sunlight with the exact truth that in painting objects in shadow the palette can compass.

Nothing is more simple. Take a landscape with a cloudy sky, which means diffused light in the old sense of the term, and observe the effect upon it of a sudden burst of sunlight. What is the effect where considerable portions of the scene are suddenly thrown into marked shadow, as well as others illuminated with intense light? Is the absolute value of the parts in shadow lowered or raised? Raised, of course, by reflected light. Formerly, to get the contrast between sunlight and shadow in proper scale, the painter would have painted the shadows darker than they were before the sun appeared. Relatively they are darker, since their value, though heightened, is raised infinitely less than the value of the parts in sunlight. Absolutely, their value is raised considerably. If, therefore, they are painted lighter than they were before the sun appeared, they in themselves seem truer. The part of Monet's picture that is in shadow is measurably true, far truer than it would have been if painted under the old theory of correspondence, and had been unnaturally darkened to express the relation of contrast between shadow and sunlight. Scale has been lost. What has been gained? Simply truth of impressionistic effect. Why? Because we know and judge and appreciate and feel the measure of truth with which objects in shadow are represented; we are insensibly more familiar with them in nature than with objects directly sun-illuminated, the value as well as the definition of which are far vaguer to us on account of their blending and infinite heightening by a luminosity absolutely overpowering. In a word, in sunlit landscapes objects in shadow are what customarily and unconsciously we see and note and know, and the illusion is greater if the relation between them and the objects in sunlight, whose value habitually we do not note, be neglected or falsified. Add to this source of illusion the success of Monet in giving a juster value to the sunlit half of his picture than had even been systematically attempted before his time, and his astonishing *trompe-l'oeil* is, I think, explained. Each part is truer than ever before, and unless one have a specially developed sense of *ensemble* in this very special matter of values in and affected by sunlight, one gets from Monet an impression of actuality so much greater than he has ever got before, that he may be pardoned for feeling, and even for enthusiastically proclaiming, that in Monet realism finds its apogee. To sum up: The first realists painted *relative* values; Manet and his derivatives painted *absolute* values, but in a wisely limited gamut; Monet paints ***absolute values in a very wide range, plus sunlight, as nearly as he can get it***--as nearly as pigment can be got to represent it. Perforce he loses scale, and therefore artistic completeness, but he secures an incomparably vivid effect of reality, of nature--and of nature in her gayest, most inspiring manifestation, illuminated directly and indirectly, and everywhere vibrant and palpitating with the light of all our physical seeing.

Monet is so subtle in his own way, so superbly successful within his own limits, that it is time wasted to quarrel with the convention-steeped philistine who refuses to comprehend even his point of view, who judges the pictures he sees by the pictures he has seen. He has not only discovered a new way of looking at nature, but he has justified it in a thousand particulars. Concentrated as his attention has been upon the effects of light and atmosphere, he has reproduced an infinity of nature's moods that are charming in proportion to their transitoriness, and whose fleeting beauties he has caught and permanently fixed. Rousseau made the most careful studies, and then combined them in his studio. Courbet made his sketch, more or less perfect, face to face with his subject, and elaborated it afterward away from it. Corot painted his picture from nature, but put the Corot into it in his studio. Monet's practice is in comparison drastically thorough. After thirty minutes, he says-- why thirty instead of forty or twenty, I do not know; these mysteries are Eleusinian to the mere amateur--the light changes; he must stop and return the next day at the same hour. The result is immensely real, and in Monet's hands immensely varied. One may say as much, having regard to their differing degrees of success, of Pissaro, who influenced him, and of Caillebotte, Renoir, Sisley, and the rest of the impressionists who followed him.

He is himself the prominent representative of the school, however, and the fact that one representative of it is enough to consider, is eloquent of profound criticism of it. For decorative purposes a hole in one's wall, an additional window through which one may only look satisfactorily during a period of thirty minutes, has its drawbacks. A walk in the country or in a city park is after all preferable to anyone who can really appreciate a Monet--that is, anyone who can feel the illusion of nature which it is his sole aim to produce. After all, what one asks of art is something different from imitative illusion. Its essence is illusion, I think, but illusion taken in a different sense from optical illusion-- *trompe-l'oeil*. Its function is to make dreams seem real, not to recall reality. Monet is enduringly admirable mainly to the painter who envies and endeavors to imitate his wonderful power of technical expression--the thing that occupies most the conscious attention of the true painter. To others he must remain a little unsatisfactory, because he is not only not a dreamer, but because he does nothing with his material except to show it as it is--a great service surely, but largely excluding the exercise of that architectonic faculty, personally directed, which is the very life of every truly aesthetic production.

VII

In fine, the impressionist has his own conventions; no school can escape them, from the very nature of the case and the definition of the term. The conventions of the impressionists, indeed, are particularly salient. Can anyone doubt it who sees an exhibition of their works? In the same number of classic, or romantic, or merely realistic pictures, is there anything quite equalling the monotony that strikes one in a display of canvasses by Claude Monet and his fellows and followers? But the defect of impressionism is not mainly its technical conventionality. It is, as I think everyone except its thick-and-thin advocates must feel, that pursued *a outrance* it lacks a seriousness commensurate with its claims--that it exhibits indeed a kind of undertone of frivolity that is all the nearer to the absolutely comic for the earnestness, so to speak, of its unconsciousness. The reason is, partly no doubt, to be ascribed to its *debonnaire* self-satisfaction, its disposition to "lightly run amuck at an august thing," the traditions of centuries namely, to its bumptiousness, in a word. But chiefly, I think, the reason is to be found in its lack of anything properly to be called a philosophy. This is surely a fatal flaw in any system, because it involves a contradiction in terms; and to say that to have no philosophy is the philosophy of the impressionists, is merely a word-juggling bit of question-begging. A theory of technic is not a philosophy, however systematic it may be. It is a mechanical, not an intellectual, point of view. It is not a way of looking at things, but of rendering them. It expresses no idea and sees no relations; its claims on one's interest are exhausted when once its right to its method is admitted. The remark once made of a typically literal person--that he cared so much for facts that he disliked to think they had any relations--is intimately applicable to the whole impressionist school. Technically, of course, the impressionist's relations are extremely just--not exquisite, but exquisitely just. But merely to get just values is not to occupy one's self with values ideally, emotionally, personally. It is merely to record facts. Certainly any impressionist rendering of the light and shade and color relations of objects seems eloquent beside any traditional and conventional rendering of them; but it is because each object is so carefully observed, so truly painted, that its relation to every other is spontaneously satisfactory; and this is a very different thing from the result of truly pictorial rendering with its constructive appeal, its sense of *ensemble*, its presentation of an idea by means of the convergence and interdependence of objects focussed to a common and central effect. To this impressionism is absolutely insensitive. It is the acme of detachment, of indifference.

Turgenieff, according to Mr. George Moore, complained of Zola's Gervaise Coupeau, that Zola explained how she felt, never what she thought. "Qu'est que ca me fait si elle suait sous les bras, ou au milieu du dos?" he asked, with most pertinent penetration. He is quite right. Really we only care for facts when they explain truths. The desultory agglomeration of never so definitely rendered details necessarily leaves the civilized appreciation cold. What distinguishes the civilized from the savage appreciation is the passion for order. The tendency to order, said Senancour, should form "an essential part of our inclinations, of our instinct, like the tendencies to self-preservation and to reproduction." The two latter tendencies the savage possesses as completely as the civilized man, but he does not share the civilized man's instinct for correlation. And in this sense, I think, a certain savagery is justly to be ascribed to the impressionist. His productions have many attractions and many merits--merits and attractions that the traditional painting has not. But they are really only by a kind of automatic inadvertence, pictures. They are not truly pictorial.

And a picture should be something more than even pictorial. To be permanently attaching it should give at least a hint of the painter's philosophy--his point of view, his attitude toward his material. In the great pictures you can not only discover this attitude, but the attitude of the painter toward life and the world in general. Everyone has as distinct an idea of the philosophy of Raphael as of the qualities of his designs. The impressionist not only does not show you what he thinks, he does not even show you how he feels, except by betraying a fondness for violets and diffused light, and by exhibiting the temper of the radical and the rioter. The order of a blithe, idyllic landscape by Corot, of one of Delacroix's pieces of concentric coloration, of an example of Ingres's purity of outline, shows not only temperament, but the position of the painter in regard to the whole intellectual world so far as he touches it at all. What does a canvas of Claude Monet show in this respect? It is more truthful but not less impersonal than a photograph.

Degas is the only other painter usually classed with the impressionists, of whom this may not be said. But Degas is hardly an impressionist at all. He is one of the most personal painters, if not the most personal painter, of the day. He is as original as Puvis de Chavannes. What allies him with the impressionists is his fondness for fleeting aspects, his caring for nothing beyond aspect--for the look of things and their transitory look. He is an enthusiastic admirer of Ingres--who, one would say, is the antithesis of impressionism. He never paints from nature. His studies are made with the utmost care, but they are arranged, composed, combined by his own sense of what is pictorial--by, at any rate, his own idea of the effects he wishes to create. He cares absolutely nothing for what ordinarily we understand by the real, the actual, so far as its reality is concerned; he sees nothing else, to be sure, and is probably very sceptical about anything but colors and shapes and their decorative arrangement; but he sees what he likes in reality and follows this out with an inerrancy so scrupulous, and even affectionate, as to convey the idea that in his result he himself counts for almost nothing. This at least may be said of him, that he shows what, given genius, can be got out of the impressionist method artistically and practically employed to the end of illustrating a personal point of view. A mere amateur can hardly distinguish between a Caillebotte and a Sisley, for example, but everyone identifies a Degas as immediately and as certainly as he does a Whistler. His work is perfectly sincere and admirably intelligent. It has neither the pose nor the irresponsibility of the impressionists. His artistic apotheosis of the ballet-girl is merely the result of his happy discovery of something delightfully, and in a very true sense naturally, decorative in material that is in the highest degree artificial. His impulse is as genuine and spontaneous as if the substance upon which it is exercised were not the acme of the exotic, and already arranged with the most elaborate conventionality. Nothing indeed could be more opposed to the elementary crudity of impressionism than his distinction and refinement, which may be said to be carried to a really *fin de siecle* degree.

VIII

Whatever the painting of the future is to be, it is certain not to be the painting of Monet. For the present, no doubt, Monet is the last word in painting. To belittle him is not only whimsical, but ridiculous. He has plainly worked a revolution in his art. He has taken it out of the vicious circle of conformity to, departure from, and return to abstractions and the so-called ideal. No one hereafter who attempts the representation of nature--and for as far ahead as we can see with any confidence, the representation of nature, the pantheistic ideal if one chooses, will increasingly intrench itself as the painter's true aim--no one who seriously attempts to realize this aim of now universal appeal will be able to dispense with Monet's aid. He must perforce follow the lines laid down for him by this astonishing naturalist. Any other course must result in solecism, and if anything future is certain, it is certain that the future will be not only inhospitable to, but absolutely intolerant of, solecism. Henceforth the basis of things is bound to be solid and not superficial, real and not fantastic. But--whether the future is to commit itself wholly to prose, or is to preserve in new conditions the essence of the poetry that, in one form or another, has persisted since plastic art began--for the superstructure to be erected on the sound basis of just values and true impressions it is justifiably easy to predict a greater interest and a more real dignity than any such preoccupation with the basis of technic as Monet's can possibly have. And though, even as one says it, one has the feeling that the future is pregnant with some genius who will out-Monet Monet, and that painting will in some now inconceivable way have to submit hereafter to a still more rigorous standard than it does at present--I have heard the claims of binocular vision urged--at the same time the true "child of nature" may console himself with the reflection that accuracy and competence are but the accidents, at most the necessary phenomena, of what really and essentially constitutes fine art of any kind--namely, the expression of a personal conception of what is not only true but beautiful as well. In France less than anywhere else is it likely that even such a powerful force as modern realism will long dominate the constructive, the architectonic faculty, which is part of the very fibre of the French genius. The exposition and illustration of a theory believed in with a fervency to be found only among a people with whom the intelligence is the chief element and object of experiment and exercise, are a natural concomitant of mental energy and activity. But no theory holds them long in bondage. At the least, it speedily gives place to another formulation of the mutinous freedom its very acceptance creates. And the conformity that each of them in succession imposes on mediocrity is always varied and relieved by the frequent incarnations in masterful personalities of the natural national traits--of which, I think, the architectonic spirit is one of the most conspicuous. Painting will again become creative, constructive, personally expressive. Its basis having been established as scientifically impeccable, its superstructure will exhibit the taste, the elegance, the imaginative freedom, exhibited within the limits of a cultivated sense of propriety, that are an integral part of the French painter's patrimony.

IV

CLASSIC SCULPTURE

I

French sculpture naturally follows very much the same course as French painting. Its beginnings, however, are Gothic, and the Renaissance emancipated rather than created it. Italy, over which the Gothic wave passed with less disturbing effect than anywhere else, and where the Pisans were doing pure sculpture when everywhere farther north sculpture was mainly decorative and rigidly architectural, had a potent influence. But the modern phases of French sculpture have a closer relationship with the Chartres Cathedral than modern French painting has with its earliest practice; and Claux Sluters, the Burgundian Fleming who modelled the wonderful Moses Well and the tombs of Jean Sans Peur and Phillippe le Hardi at Dijon, among his other anachronistic masterpieces, exerted considerably greater influence upon his successors than the Touraine school of painting and the Clouets did upon theirs.

These works are a curious compromise between the Gothic and the modern spirits. Sluters was plainly a modern temperament working with Gothic material and amid Gothic ideas. In itself his sculpture is hardly decorative, as we apply the epithet to modern work. It is just off the line of rigidity, of insistence in every detail of its right and title to individuality apart from every other sculptured detail. The prophets in the niches of the beautiful Dijon Well, the monks under the arcades of the beautiful Burgundian tombs, have little relation with each other as elements of a decorative sculptural composition. They are in the same style, that is all. Each of them is in interest quite independent of the other. Compared with one of the

Pisans' pulpits they form a congeries rather than a composition. Compared with Goujon's "Fountain of the Innocents" their motive is not decorative at all. Isaiah, Ezekiel, Jeremiah asserts his individuality in a way the more sociable prophets of the Sistine Chapel would hesitate to do. They have a little the air of hermits--of artistic anchorites, one may say.

They are Gothic, too, not only in being thus sculpturally undecorative and un-composed, but in being beautifully subordinate to the architecture which it is their unmistakable ancillary function to decorate in the most delightful way imaginable--in being in a word architecturally decorative. The marriage of the two arts is, Gothically, not on equal terms. It never occurred, of course, to the Gothic architect that it should be. His *ensemble* was always one of which the chief, the overwhelming, one may almost say the sole, interest is structural. He even imposed the condition that the sculpture which decorated his structure should be itself architecturally structural. One figure of the portals of Chartres is almost as like another as one pillar of the interior is like its fellows; for the reason--eminently satisfactory to the architect--that it discharges an identical function.

Emancipation from this thraldom of the architect is Sluters's great distinction, however. He is modern in this sense, without going so far--without going anything like so far--as the modern sculptor who divorces his work from that of the architect with whom he is called upon to combine to the end of an *ensemble* that shall be equally agreeable to the sense satisfied by form and that satisfied by structure. His figures, subordinate as they are to the general architectural purpose and function of what they decorate, are not only not purely structural in their expression, stiff as they still are from the point of view of absolutely free sculpture; they are, moreover, not merely unrelated to each other in any essential sense, such as that in which the figures of the Pisans and of Goujon are related; they are on the contrary each and all wonderfully accentuated and individualized. Every ecclesiastic on the Dijon tombs is a character study. Every figure on the Well has a psychologic as well as a sculptural interest. Poised between Gothic tradition and modern feeling, between a reverend and august aesthetic conventionality and the dawn of free activity, Sluters is one of the most interesting and stimulating figures in the whole history of sculpture. And the force of his characterizations, the vividness of his conceptions, and the combined power and delicacy of his modelling give him the added importance of one of the heroes of his art in any time or country. There is something extremely Flemish in his sense of personality. A similar interest in humanity as such, in the individual apart from the type, is noticeable in the pictures of the Van Eycks, of Memling, of Quentin Matsys, and Roger Van der Weyden, wherein all idea of beauty, of composition, of universal appeal is subordinated as it is in no other art--in that of Holland no more than in that of Italy--to the representation in the most definite, precise, and powerful way of some intensely human personality. There is the same extraordinary concreteness in one of Matsys's apostles and one of Sluters's prophets.

Michel Colombe, the pupil of Claux and Anthoniet and the sculptor of the monument of Francois II., Duke of Brittany, at Nantes, the relief of "St. George and the Dragon" for the Chateau of Gaillon, now in the Louvre, and the Fontaine de Beaune, at Tours, and Jean Juste, whose noble masterpiece, the Tomb of Louis XII. and Anne of Brittany, is the finest ornament of the Cathedral of St. Denis, bridge the distance and mark the transition to Goujon, Cousin, and Germain Pilon far more suavely than the school of Fontainebleau did the change from that of Tours to Poussin. Cousin, though the monument of Admiral Chabot is a truly marvellous work, witnessing a practical sculptor's hand, is really to be classed among painters. And Germain Pilon's compromise with Italian decorativeness, graceful and fertile sculptor as his many works show him to have been, resulted in a lack of personal force that has caused him to be thought on the one hand "seriously injured by the bastard sentiment proper to the school of Fontainebleau," as Mrs. Pattison somewhat sternly remarks, and on the other to be reprehended by Germain Brice in 1718, for evincing *quelque reste du gout gothique* --some reminiscence of Gothic taste. Jean Goujon is really the first modern French sculptor.

II

He remains, too, one of the very finest, even in a competition constantly growing more exacting since his day. He had a very particular talent, and it was exhibited in manifold ways. He is as fine in relief as in the round. His decorative quality is as eminent as his purely sculptural side. Compared with his Italian contemporaries he is at once full of feeling and severe. He has nothing of Pilon's chameleon-like imitativeness. He does not, on the other hand, break with the traditions of the best models known to him--and, undoubtedly he knew the best. His works cover and line the Louvre, and anyone who visits Paris may get a perfect conception of his genius--certainly anyone who in addition visits Rouen and beholds the lovely tracery of his earliest sculpture on the portal of St. Maclou. He was eminently the sculptor of an educated class, and appealed to a cultivated appreciation. Coming as he did at the acme of the French Renaissance, when France was borrowing with intelligent selection whatever it considered valuable from Italy, he pleased the dilettanti. There is something distinctly "swell" in his work. He does not perhaps express any overmastering personal feeling, nor does he stamp the impress of French national character on his work with any particular emphasis. He is too well-bred and too cultivated, he has too much ***aplomb***. But his works show both more personal feeling and more national character than the works of his contemporaries elsewhere. For line he has a very intimate instinct, and of mass, in the sculptor's as well as the painter's sense, he has a native comprehension. Compare his "Diana" of the Louvre with Cellini's in the adjoining room from the point of view of pure sculpture. Goujon's group is superb in every way. Cellini's figure is tormented and distorted by an impulse of decadent though decorative aestheticism. Goujon's caryatides and figures of the Innocents Fountain are equally sculptural in their way--by no means arabesques, as is so much of Renaissance relief, and the modern relief that imitates it. Everything in fine that Goujon did is unified with the rest of his work and identifiable by the mark of style.

III

What do we mean by style? Something, at all events, very different from manner, in spite of Mr. Hamerton's insistence upon the contrary. Is the quality in virtue of which--as Mr. Dobson paraphrases Gautier--

"The bust outlives the throne,   The coin Tiberius"

the specific personality of the artist who carved the bust or chiselled the coin that have thus outlived all personality connected with them? Not that personality is not of the essence of enduring art. It is, on the contrary, the condition of any vital art whatever. But what gives the object, once personally conceived and expressed, its currency, its universality, its eternal interest--speaking to strangers with familiar vividness, and to posterity as to contemporaries--is something aside from its personal feeling. And it is this something and not specific personality that style is. Style is the invisible wind through whose influence "the lion on the flag" of the Persian poet "moves and marches." The lion of personality may be painted never so deftly, with never so much expression, individual feeling, picturesqueness, energy, charm; it will not move and march save through the rhythmic, waving influence of style.

Nor is style necessarily the grand style, as Arnold seems to imply, in calling it "a peculiar recasting and heightening, under a certain condition of spiritual excitement, of what a man has to say in such a manner as to add dignity and distinction to it." Perhaps the most explicit examples of pure style owe their production to spiritual coolness; and, in any event, the word "peculiar" in a definition begs the question. Buffon is at once juster and more definite in saying: "Style is nothing other than the order and movement which we put into our thoughts." It is singular that this simple and lucid utterance of Buffon should have been so little noticed by those who have written in English on style. In general English writers have apparently misconceived, in very curious fashion, Buffon's other remark, "le style c'est l'homme;" by which aphorism Buffon merely meant that a man's individual manner depends on his temperament, his character, and which he, of course, was very far from suspecting would ever be taken for a definition.

Following Buffon's idea of "order and movement," we may say, perhaps, that style results from the preservation in every part of some sense of the form of the whole. It implies a sense of relations as well as of statement. It is not mere expression of a thought in a manner peculiar to the artist (in words, color, marble, what not), but it is such expression penetrated with both reminiscence and anticipation. It is, indeed, on the contrary, very nearly the reverse of what we mean by expression, which is mainly a matter of personal energy. Style means correctness, precision, that feeling for the ***ensemble*** on which an inharmonious detail jars. Expression results from a sense of the value of the detail. If Walt Whitman, for example, were what his admirers' defective sense of style fancies him, he would be expressive. If French academic art had as little expression as its censors assert, it would still illustrate style--the quality which modifies the native and apposite form of the concrete individual thing with reference to what has preceded and what is to follow it; the quality, in a word, whose effort is to harmonize the object with its environment. When this environment is heightened, and universal instead of logical and particular, we have the "grand style;" but we have the grand style generally in poetry, and to be sure of style at all prose--such prose as Goujon's, which in no wise emulates Michael Angelo's poetry--may justifiably neglect in some degree the specific personality that tends to make it poetic and individual.

IV

After Goujon, Clodion is the great name in French sculpture, until we come to Houdon, who may almost be assigned to the nineteenth century. There were throughout the eighteenth century honorable artists, sculptors of distinction beyond contest. But sculpture is such an abstract art itself that the sculpture which partook of the artificiality of the eighteenth century has less interest for us, less that is concrete and appealing than even the painting of the epoch. It derived its canons and its practice from Puget--the French Bernini, who with less grace and less dilettante extravagance than his Italian exemplar had more force and solidity. With less cleverness, less charm--for Bernini, spite of the disesteem in which his juxtaposition to Michael Angelo and his apparent unconsciousness of the attitude such juxtaposition should have imposed upon him, cause him to be held, has a great deal of charm and is extraordinarily clever--he is more sincere, more thorough-going, more respectable. Coysevox is chiefly Puget exaggerated, and his pupil, Coustou, who comes down to nearly the middle of the eighteenth century, contributed nothing to French sculptural tradition.

But Clodion is a distinct break. He is as different from Coysevox and Coustou as Watteau is from Lebrun. He is the essence of what we mean by Louis Quinze. His work is clever beyond characterization. It has in perfection what sculptors mean by color--that is to say a certain warmth of feeling, a certain ***insouciance***, a brave carelessness for sculpturesque traditions, a free play of fancy, both in the conception and execution of his subjects. Like the Louis Quinze painters, he has his thoughtless, irresponsible, involuntary side, and like them--like the best of them, that is to say, like Watteau--he is never quite as good as he could be. He seems not so much concerned at expressing his ideal as at pleasing, and pleasing people of too frivolous an appreciation to call forth what is best in him. He devoted himself almost altogether to terra-cotta, which is equivalent to saying that the exquisite and not the impressive was his aim. Thoroughly classic, so far as the avoidance of everything naturalistic is concerned, he is yet as little severe and correct as the painters of his day. He spent nine years in Rome, but though enamoured in the most sympathetic degree of the antique, it was the statuettes and figurines, the gay and social, the elegant and decorative side of antique sculpture that exclusively he delighted in. His work is Tanagra Gallicized. It is not the group of "The Deluge," or the "Entry of the French into Munich," or "Hercules in Repose," for which he was esteemed by contemporaries or is prized by posterity. He is admirable where he is inimitable--that is to say, in the delightful decoration of which he was so prodigal. It is not in his compositions essaying what is usually meant by sculptural effect, but in his vases, clocks, pendants, volutes, little reliefs of nymphs riding dolphins over favoring breakers and amid hospitable foam, his toilettes of Venus, his facade ornamentations, his applied sculpture, in a word, that his true talent lies. After him it is natural that we should have a reversion to quasi-severity and imitation of the antique--just as David succeeded to the Louis Quinze pictorial riot--and that the French contemporaries of Canova and Thorwaldsen, those literal, though enthusiastic illustrators of Winckelmann's theories, should be Pradier and Etex and the so-called Greek school. Pradier's Greek inspiration has something Swiss about it, one may say--he was a Genevan--though his figures were simple and largely treated. He had a keen sense for the feminine element--the ***ewig Weibliche***--and expressed it plastically with a zest approaching gusto. Yet his statues are women rather than statues, and, more than that, are handsome rather than beautiful. Etex, it is to be feared, will be chiefly remembered as the unfortunately successful rival of Rude in the Arc de Triomphe de l'Etoile decoration.

V

Having in each case more or less relation with, but really wholly outside of and superior to all "schools" whatever--except the school of nature, which permits as much freedom as it exacts fidelity--is the succession of the greatest of French sculptors since the Renaissance and down to the present day: Houdon, David d'Angers, Rude, Carpeaux, and Barye. Houdon is one of the finest examples of the union of vigor with grace. He will be known chiefly as a portraitist, but such a masterpiece as his "Diana" shows how admirable he was in the sphere of purely imaginative theme and treatment. Classic, and even conventionally classic as it is, both in subject and in the way the subject is handled--compared for example with M. Falguiere's "Nymph Hunting," which is simply a realistic Diana--it is designed and modelled with as much personal freedom and feeling as if Houdon had been stimulated by the ambition of novel accomplishment, instead of that of rendering with truth and grace a time-honored and traditional sculptural motive. Its treatment is beautifully educated and its effect refined, chaste, and elevated in an extraordinary degree. No master ever steered so near the reef of "clock-tops," one may say, and avoided it so surely and triumphantly. The figure is light as air and wholly effortless at the same time. There has rarely been such a distinguished success in circumventing the great difficulty of sculpture--which is to rob marble or metal of its specific gravity and make it appear light and buoyant, just as the difficulty of the painter is to give weight and substance to his fictions. But Houdon's admirable busts of Moliere, Diderot, Washington, Franklin, and Mirabeau, his unequalled statue of Voltaire in the *foyer* of the Francais and his San Bruno in Santa Maria degli Angeli at Rome are the works on which his fame will chiefly rest, and, owing to their masterly combination of strength with style, rest securely.

To see the work of David d'Angers, one must go to Angers itself and to Pere-Lachaise. The Louvre is lamentably lacking in anything truly representative of this most eminent of all portraitists in sculpture, I think, not excepting even Houdon, if one may reckon the mass as well as the excellence of his remarkable production and the way in which it witnesses that portraiture is just what he was born to do. The "Philopoemen" of the Louvre is a fine work, even impressively large and simple. But it is the competent work of a member of a school and leaves one a little cold. Its academic quality quite overshadows whatever personal feeling one may by searching find in the severity of its treatment and the way in which a classic motive has been followed out naturally and genuinely instead of perfunctorily. It gives no intimation of the faculty that produced the splendid gallery of medallions accentuated by an occasional bust and statue, of David's celebrated contemporaries and quasi-contemporaries in every field of distinction. It is impossible to overestimate the interest and value, the truth and the art of these. Whether the subject be intractable or not seems to have made no difference to David. He invariably produced a work of art at the same time that he expressed the character of its motive with uncompromising fidelity. His portraits, moreover, are pure sculpture. There is nothing of the cameo-cutter's art about them. They are modelled not carved. The outline is no more important than it is in nature, so far as it is employed to the end of identification. It is used decoratively. There are surprising effects of fore-shortening, exhibiting superb, and as it were unconscious ease in handling relief--that most difficult of illusions in respect of having no law (at least no law that it is worth the sculptor's while to try to discover) of correspondence to reality. Forms and masses have a definition and a firmness wholly remarkable in their independence of the usual low relief's reliance on pictorial and purely linear design. They do not blend picturesquely with the background, and do not depend on their suggestiveness for their character. They are always realized, executed--sculpture in a word whose suggestiveness, quite as potent as that of feebler executants, begins only when actual representation has been triumphantly achieved instead of impotently and skilfully avoided.

Of Rude's genius one's first thought is of its robustness, its originality. Everything he did is stamped with the impress of his personality. At the same time it is equally evident that Rude's own temperament took its color from the transitional epoch in which he lived, and of which he was *par excellence* the sculptor. He was the true inheritor of his Burgundian traditions. His strongest side was that which allies him with his artistic ancestor, Claux Sluters. But he lived in an era of general culture and aestheticism, and all his naturalistic tendencies were complicated with theory. He accepted the antique not merely as a stimulus, but as a model. He was not only a sculptor but a teacher, and the formulation of his didacticism complicated considerably the free exercise of his expression. At the last, as is perhaps natural, he reverted to precedent and formulary, and in his "Hebe and the Eagle of Jupiter" and his "L'Amour Dominateur du Monde," is more at variance than anywhere else with his native instinct, which was, to cite the admirable phrase of M. de Fourcaud, *extérioriser nos idées et nos ames*. But throughout his life he halted a little between two opinions--the current admiration of the classic, and his own instinctive feeling for nature unsystematized and unsophisticated. His "Jeanne d'Arc" is an instance. In spite of the violation of tradition, which at the time it was thought to be, it seems to-day to our eyes to err on the side of the conventional. It is surely intellectual, classic, even factitious in conception as well as in execution. In some of its accessories it is even modish. It illustrates not merely the abstract turn of conceiving a subject which Rude always shared with the great classicists of his art, but also the arbitrariness of treatment against which he always protested. Without at all knowing it, he was in a very intimate sense an eclectic in many of his works. He believed in forming a complete mental conception of every composition before even posing a model, as he used to tell his students, but in complicated compositions this was impossible, and he had small talent for artificial composition. Furthermore, he often distrusted--quite without reason, but after the fatal manner of the rustic--his own intuitions. But one mentions these qualifications of his genius and accomplishment only because both his genius and accomplishment are so distinguished as to make one wish they were more nearly perfect than they are. It is really idle to wish that Rude had neglected the philosophy of his art, with which he was so much occupied, and had devoted himself exclusively to treating sculptural subjects in the manner of a nineteenth century successor of Sluters and Anthoniet. He might have been a greater sculptor than he was, but he is sufficiently great as he is. If his "Mercury" is an essay in conventional sculpture, his "Petit Pecheur" is frank and free sculptural handling of natural material. His work at Lille and in Belgium, his reclining figure of Cavaignac in the cemetery of Montmartre, his noble figures of Gaspard Monge at Beaune, of Marshal Bertrand, and of Ney, are all cast in the heroic mould, full of character, and in no wise dependent on speculative theory. Few sculptors have displayed anything like his variety and range, which extends, for example, from the "Baptism of Christ" to a statue of "Louis XIII. enfant," and includes portraits, groups, compositions in relief, and heroic statues. In all his successful work one cannot fail to note the force and fire of the man's personality, and perhaps what one thinks of chiefly in connection with him is the misfortune which we owe to the vacillation of M. Thiers of having but one instead of four groups by him on the piers of the Arc de Triomphe de l'Etoile. Carpeaux used to say that he never passed the "Chant du Depart" without taking off his hat. One can understand his feeling. No one can have any appreciation of what sculpture is without perceiving that this magnificent group easily and serenely takes its rank among the masterpieces of sculpture of all time. It is, in the first place, the incarnation of an abstraction, the spirit of patriotism roused to the highest pitch of warlike intensity and self-sacrifice, and in the second this abstract motive is expressed in the most elaborate and comprehensive completeness--with a combined intricacy of detail and singleness of effect which must be the despair of any but a master in sculpture.

VI

Carpeaux perhaps never did anything that quite equals the masterpiece of his master Rude. But the essential quality of the "Chant du Depart" he assimilated so absolutely and so naturally that he made it in a way his own. He carried it farther, indeed. If he never rose to the grandeur of this superb group, and he certainly did not, he nevertheless showed in every one of his works that he was possessed by its inspiration even more completely than was Rude himself. His passion was the representation of life, the vital and vivifying force in its utmost exuberance, and in its every variety, so far as his experience could enable him to render it. He was infatuated with movement, with the attestation in form of nervous energy, of the quick translation of thought and emotion into interpreting attitude. His figures are, beyond all others, so thoroughly alive as to seem conscious of the fact and joy of pure existence. They are animated, one may almost say inspired, with the delight of muscular activity, the sensation of exercising the functions with which nature endows them. And accompanying this supreme motive and effect is a delightful grace and winningness of which few sculptors have the secret, and which suggest more than any one else Clodion's decorative loveliness. An even greater charm of sprite-like, fairy attractiveness, of caressing and bewitching fascination, a more penetrating and seductive engagingness plays about Carpeaux's "Flora," I think, than is characteristic even of Clodion's figures and reliefs. Carpeaux is at all events nearer to us, and if he has not the classic detachment of Clodion he substitutes for it a quality of closer attachment and more intimate appeal. He is at his best perhaps in the "Danse" of the Nouvel Opera facade, wherein his elfin-like grace and exuberant vitality animate a group carefully, and even classically composed, exhibiting skill and restraint as well as movement and fancy. Possibly his temperament gives itself too free a rein in the group of the Luxembourg Gardens, in which he has been accused by his own admirers of sacrificing taste to turbulence and securing expressiveness at the expense of saner and more truly sculptural aims. But fancy the Luxembourg Gardens without "The Four Quarters of the World supporting the Earth." Parisian censure of his exuberance is very apt to display a conventional standard of criticism in the critic rather than to substantiate its charge.

Barye's place in the history of art is more nearly unique, perhaps, than that of any of the great artists. He was certainly one of the greatest of sculptors, and he had either the good luck or the mischance to do his work in a field almost wholly unexploited before him. He has in his way no rivals, and in his way he is so admirable that the scope of his work does not even hint at his exclusion from rivalry with the very greatest of his predecessors. A perception of the truth of this apparent paradox is the nearest one may come, I think, to the secret of his excellence. No matter what you do, if you do it well enough, that is, with enough elevation, enough spiritual distinction, enough transmutation of the elementary necessity of technical perfection into true significance--you succeed. And this is not the sense in which motive in art is currently belittled. It is rather the suggestion of Mrs. Browning's lines:

> "Better far　Pursue a frivolous trade by serious means　Than a sublime art frivolously."

Nothing could be more misleading than to fancy Barye a kind of modern Cellini. Less than any sculptor of modern times is he a decorative artist. The small scale of his works is in great part due to his lack of opportunity to produce larger ones. Nowadays one does what one can, even the greatest artists; and Barye had no Lorenzo de'Medici for a patron, but, instead, a frowning Institute, which confined him to such work as, in the main, he did. He did it ***con amore*** it need not be added, and thus lifted it at once out of the customary category of such work. His bronzes were never ***articles de Paris***, and their excellence transcends the function of teaching our sculptors and amateurs the lesson that "household" is as dignified a province as monumental, art. His groups are not essentially "clock-tops," and the work of perhaps the greatest artist, in the line from Jean Goujon to Carpeaux can hardly be used to point the moral that "clock-tops" ought to be good. Cellini's "Perseus" is really more of a "parlor ornament" than Barye's smallest figure.

Why is he so obviously great as well as so obviously extraordinary? one constantly asks himself in the presence of his bronzes. Perhaps because he expresses with such concreteness, such definiteness and vigor a motive so purely an abstraction. The illustration in intimate elaboration of elemental force, strength, passion, seems to have been his aim, and in everyone of his wonderfully varied groups he attains it superbly--not giving the beholder a symbol of it merely; in no degree depending upon association or convention, but exhibiting its very essence with a combined scientific explicitness and poetic energy to which antique art alone, one may almost say, has furnished a parallel. For this, fauna served him as well as the human figure, though, could he have studied man with the facility which the Jardin des Plantes afforded him of observing the lower animals, he might have used the medium of the human figure more frequently than he did. When he did, he was hardly less successful; and the four splendid groups that decorate the Pavillons Denon and Richelieu of the Louvre are in the very front rank of the heroic sculpture of the modern world.

V

ACADEMIC SCULPTURE
I

From Barye to the Institute is a long way. Nothing could be more interhostile than his sculpture and that of the professors at the Ecole des Beaux-Arts. And in considering the French sculpture of the present day we may say that, aside from the great names already mentioned--Houdon, David d'Angers, Rude, Carpeaux, and Barye--and apart from the new movement represented by Rodin and Dalou, it is represented by the Institute, and that the Institute has reverted to the Italian inspiration. The influence of Canova and the example of Pradier and Etex were not lasting. Indeed, Greek sculpture has perished so completely that it sometimes seems to live only in its legend. With the modern French school, the academic school, it is quite supplanted by the sculpture of the Renaissance. And this is not unreasonable. The Renaissance sculpture is modern; its masters did finely and perfectly what since their time has been done imperfectly, but essentially its artistic spirit is the modern artistic spirit, full of personality, full of expression, careless of the type. Nowadays we patronize a little the ideal. You may hear very intelligent critics in Paris--who in Paris is not an intelligent critic?--speak disparagingly of the Greek want of expression; of the lack of passion, of vivid interest, of significance in a word, in Greek sculpture of the Periclean epoch. The conception of absolute beauty having been discovered to be an abstraction, the tradition of the purely ideal has gone with it. The caryatids of the Erechtheum, the horsemen of the Parthenon frieze, the reliefs of the Nike Apteros balustrade are admired certainly; but they are hardly sympathetically admired; there is a tendency to relegate them to the limbo of subjects for aesthetic lectures. And yet no one can have carefully examined the brilliant productions of modern French sculpture without being struck by this apparent paradox: that, whereas all its canons are drawn from a study of the Renaissance, its chief characteristic is, at bottom, a lack of expression, a carefulness for the type. The explanation is this: in the course of time, which "at last makes all things even," the individuality, the romanticism of the Renaissance has itself become the type, is now itself become "classical," and the modern attitude toward it, however sympathetic compared with the modern attitude toward the antique, is to a noteworthy degree factitious and artificial. And in art everything depends upon the attitude of mind. It is this which prevents Ingres from being truly Raphaelesque, and Pradier from being really classical. If, therefore, it can justly be said of modern French sculpture that its sympathy for the Renaissance sculpture obscures its vision of the ideal, it is clearly to be charged with the same absence of individual significance with which its thick-and-thin partisans reproach the antique. The circumstance that, like the Renaissance sculpture, it deals far more largely in pictorial expression than the antique does, is, if it deals in them after the Renaissance fashion and not after a fashion of its own, quite beside the essential fact. There is really nothing in common between an academic French sculptor of the present day and an Italian sculptor of the fifteenth century, except the possession of what is called the modern spirit. But the modern spirit manifests itself in an enormous gamut, and the differences of its manifestations are as great in their way, and so far as our interest in them is concerned, as the difference between their inspiration and the mediaeval or the antique inspiration.

II

Chapu, who died a year or two ago, is perhaps the only eminent sculptor of the time whose inspiration is clearly the antique, and when I add that his work appears to me for this reason none the less original, it will be immediately perceived that I share imperfectly the French objection to the antique. Indeed, nowadays to have the antique inspiration is to be original *ex vi termini*; nothing is farther removed from contemporary conventions. But this is true in a much more integral sense.

The pre-eminent fact of Greek sculpture, for example, is, from one point of view, the directness with which it concerns itself with the ideal--the slight temporary or personal element with which it is alloyed. When one calls an artist or a work Greek, this is what is really meant; it is the sense in which Raphael is Greek. Chapu is Greek in this way, and thus individualized among his contemporaries, not only by having a different inspiration from them, but by depending for his interest on no convention fixed or fleeting and on no indirect support of accentuated personal characteristics. Perhaps the antiquary of a thousand years from now, to whom the traits which to us distinguish so clearly the work of certain sculptors who seem to have nothing in common will betray only their common inspiration, will be even less at a loss than ourselves to find traces of a common origin in such apparently different works as Chapu's "Mercury" and his "Jeunesse" of the Regnault monument. He will by no means confound these with the classical productions of M. Millet or M. Cavelier, we may be sure. And this, I repeat, because their purely Greek spirit, the subordination in their conception and execution of the personal element, the direct way in which the sculptor looks at the ideal, the type, not only distinguish them among contemporary works, which are so largely personal expressions, but give them an eminent individuality as well. Like the Greek sculpture, they are plainly the production of culture, which in restraining wilfulness, however happily inspired, and imposing measure and poise, nevertheless acutely stimulates and develops the faculties themselves. The skeptic who may very plausibly inquire the distinction between that vague entity, "the ideal," and the personal idea of the artist concerned with it, can be shown this distinction better than it can be expressed in words. He will appreciate it very readily, to return to Chapu, by contrasting the "Jeanne d'Arc" at the Luxembourg Gallery with such different treatment of the same theme as M. Bastien-Lepage's picture, now in the New York Metropolitan Museum, illustrates. Contrary to his almost invariable practice of neglecting even design in favor of impersonal natural representation, Bastien-Lepage's "Jeanne d'Arc" is the creature of wilful originality, a sort of embodied protest against conventionalism in historical painting; she is the illustration of a theory, she is this and that systematically and not spontaneously; the predominance of the painter's personality is plain in every detail of his creation. Chapu's "Maid" is the ideal, more or less perfectly expressed; she is everybody's "Maid," more or less adequately embodied. The statue is the antipodes of the conventional much more so, even, to our modern sense, than that of Rude; it suggests no competition with that at Versailles or the many other characterless conceptions that abound. It is full of expression--arrested just before it ceases to be suggestive; of individuality restrained on the hither side of peculiarity. The "Maid" is hearing her "voices" as distinctly as Bastien-Lepage's figure is, but the fact is not forced upon the sense, but is rather disclosed to the mind with great delicacy and the dignity becoming sculpture. No one could, of course, mistake this work for an antique--an error that might possibly be made, supposing the conditions favorable, in the case of Chapu's "Mercury;" but it presents, nevertheless, an excellent illustration of a modern working naturally and freely in the antique spirit. It is as affecting, as full of direct appeal, as a modern work essays to be; but its appeal is to the sense of beauty, to the imagination, and its effect is wrought in virtue of its art and not of its reality. No, individuality is no more inconsistent with the antique spirit than it is with eccentricity, with the extravagances of personal expression. Is there more individuality in a thirteenth-century grotesque than in the "Faun" of the Capitol? For sculpture especially, art is eminently, as it has been termed, "the discipline of genius," and it is only after the sculptor's genius has submitted to the discipline of culture that it evinces an individuality which really counts, which is really thrown out in relief on the background of crude personality. And if there be no question of perfection, but only of the artist's attitude, one has but to ask himself the real meaning of the epithet Shakespearian to be assured of the harmony between individuality and the most impersonal practice.

Nevertheless, this attitude and this perfection, characteristic as they are of Chapu's work, have their peril. When the quickening impulse, of whose expression they are after all but conditions, fails, they suddenly appear so misplaced as to render insignificant what would otherwise have seemed "respectable" enough work. Everywhere else of great distinction--even in the execution of so perfunctory a task as a commission for a figure of "Mechanical Art" in the Tribunal de Commerce--at the great Triennial Exposition of 1883 Chapu was simply insignificant. There was never a more striking illustration of the necessity of constant renewal of inspiration, of the constant danger of lapse into the perfunctory and the hackneyed, which threatens an artist of precisely Chapu's qualities. Another of equal eminence escapes this peril; there is not the same interdependence of form and "content" to be disturbed by failure in the latter; or, better still, the merits of form are not so distinguished as to require imperatively a corresponding excellence of intention. In fact, it is because of the exceptional position that he occupies in deriving from the antique, instead of showing the academic devotion to Renaissance romanticism which characterizes the general movement of academic French sculpture, that in any consideration of this sculpture Chapu's work makes a more vivid impression than that of his contemporaries, and thus naturally takes a foremost place.

III

M. Paul Dubois, for example, in the characteristics just alluded to, presents the greatest possible contrast to Chapu; but he will never, we may be sure, give us a work that could be called insignificant. His work will always express himself, and his is a personality of very positive idiosyncrasy. M. Dubois, indeed, is probably the strongest of the Academic group of French sculptors of the day. The tomb of General Lamoriciere at Nantes has remained until recently one of the very finest achievements of sculpture in modern times. There is in effect nothing markedly superior in the Cathedral of St. Denis, which is a great deal to say--much more, indeed, than the glories of the Italian Renaissance, which lead us out of mere momentum to forget the French, permit one to appreciate. Indeed, the sculpture of M. Dubois seems positively to have but one defect, a defect which from one point of view is certainly a quality, the defect of impeccability. It is at any rate impeccable; to seek in it a blemish, or, within its own limitations, a distinct shortcoming, is to lose one's pains. As workmanship, and workmanship of the subtler kind, in which every detail of surface and structure is perceived to have been intelligently felt (though rarely enthusiastically rendered), it is not merely satisfactory, but visibly and beautifully perfect. But in the category in which M. Dubois is to be placed that is very little; it is always delightful, but it is not especially complimentary to M. Dubois, to occupy one's self with it. On the other hand, by impeccability is certainly not here meant the mere success of expressing what one has to express--the impeccability of Canova and his successors, for example. The difficulty is with M. Dubois's ideal, with what he so perfectly expresses. In the last analysis this is not his ideal more than ours. And this, indeed, is what makes his work so flawless in our eyes, so impeccable. It seems as if of what he attempts he attains the type itself; everyone must recognize its justness.

The reader will say at once here that I am cavilling at M. Dubois for what I praised in Chapu. But let us distinguish. The two artists belong to wholly different categories. Chapu's inspiration is the antique spirit. M. Dubois, is, like all academic French sculptors, except Chapu indeed, absolutely and integrally a romanticist, completely enamoured of the Renaissance. The two are so distinct as to be contradictory. The moment M. Dubois gives us the *type* in a "Florentine Minstrel," to the exclusion of the personal and the particular, he fails in imaginativeness and falls back on the conventional. The *type* of a "Florentine Minstrel" is infallibly a convention. M. Dubois, not being occupied directly with the ideal, is bound to carry his subject and its idiosyncrasies much farther than the observer could have foreseen. To rest content with expressing gracefully and powerfully the notion common to all connoisseurs is to fall short of what one justly exacts of the romantic artist. Indeed, in exchange for this one would accept very faulty work in this category with resignation. Whatever we may say or think, however we may admire or approve, in romantic art the quality that charms, that fascinates, is not adequacy but unexpectedness. In addition to the understanding, the instinct demands satisfaction. The virtues of "Charity" and "Faith" and the ideas of "Military Courage" and "Meditation" could not be more adequately illustrated than by the figures which guard the solemn dignity of General Lamoriciere's sleep. There is a certain force, a breadth of view in the general conception, something in the way in which the sculptor has taken his task, closely allied to real grandeur. The confident and even careless dependence upon the unaided value of its motive, making hardly any appeal to the fancy on the one hand, and seeking no poignant effect on the other, endues the work with the poise and purity of effortless strength. It conveys to the mind a clear impression of manliness, of qualities morally refreshing.

But such work educates us so inexorably, teaches us to be so exacting! After enjoying it to its and our utmost, we demand still something else, something more moving, more stirring, something more directly appealing to our impulse and instinct. Even in his free and charming little "St. John Baptist" of the Luxembourg, and his admirable bust of Baudry one feels like asking for more freedom still, for more "swing." Dubois certainly is the last artist who needs to be on his guard against "letting himself go." Why is it that in varying so agreeably Renaissance themes--compare the "Military Courage" and Michael Angelo's "Pensiero," or the "Charity" and the same group in Della Quercia's fountain at Sienna--it is restraint, rather than audacity, that governs him? Is it caution or perversity? In a word, imaginativeness is what permanently interests and attaches, the imaginativeness to which in sculpture the ordinary conventions of form are mere conditions, and the ordinary conventions of idea mere material. One can hardly apply generalities of the kind to M. Dubois without saying too much, but it is nevertheless true that one may illustrate the grand style and yet fail of being intimately and acutely sympathetic; and M. Dubois, to whose largeness of treatment and nobility of conception no one will deny something truly suggestive of the grand style, does thus fail. It is not that he does not possess charm, and charm in no mean proportion to his largeness and nobility, but for the elevation of these into the realm of magic, into the upper air of spontaneous spiritual activity, his imagination has, for the romantic imagination which it is, a trifle too much self-possession--too much sanity, if one chooses. He has the ambitions, the faculties, of a lyric poet, and he gives us too frequently recitative.

IV

It is agreeable in many ways to turn from the rounded and complete impeccability of M. Dubois to the fancy of M. Saint-Marceaux. More than any of his rivals, M. Saint-Marceaux possesses the charm of unexpectedness. He is not perhaps to be called an original genius, and his work will probably leave French sculpture very nearly where it found it. Indeed, one readily perceives that he is not free from the trammels of contemporary convention. But how easily he wears them, and if no "severe pains and birth-throes" accompany the evolution of his conceptions, how graceful these conceptions are! They are perhaps of the Canova family; the "Harlequin," for instance, which has had such a prodigious success, is essentially Milanese sculpture; essentially even the "Genius Guarding the Secret of the Tomb" is a fantastic rather than an original work. But how the manner, the treatment, triumphs over the Canova insipidity! It is not only Milanese sculpture better done, the execution beautifully sapient and truthful instead of cheaply imitative, the idea broadly enforced by the details instead of frittered away among them; it is Milanese sculpture essentially elevated and dignified. Loosely speaking, the mere ***article de vertu*** becomes a true work of art. And this transformation, or rather this development of a germ of not too great intrinsic importance, is brought about in the work of Saint-Marceaux by the presence of an element utterly foreign to the Canova sculpture and its succession--the element of character. If to the clever workmanship of the Italians he merely opposed workmanship of a superior kind as well as quality--thoroughly artistic workmanship, that is to say--his sculpture would be far less interesting than it is. He does, indeed, noticeably do this; there is a felicity entirely delightful, almost magical, in every detail of his work. But when one compares it with the sculpture of M. Dubois, it is not of this that one thinks so much as of a certain individual character with which M. Saint-Marceaux always contrives to endue it. This is not always in its nature sculptural, it must be admitted, and it approaches perhaps too near the character of ***genre*** to have the enduring interest that purely sculptural qualities possess. But it is always individual, piquant, and charming, and in it consists M. Saint-Marceaux's claim upon us as an artist. No one else, even given his powers of workmanship, that is to say as perfectly equipped as he, could have treated so thoroughly conventional a ***genre*** subject as the "Harlequin" as he has treated it. The mask is certainly one of the stock properties of the subject, but notice how it is used to confer upon the whole work a character of mysterious witchery. It is as a whole, if you choose, an ***article de Paris***, with the distinction of being seriously treated; the modelling and the movement admirable as far as they go, but well within the bounds of that anatomically artistic expression which is the ***raison d'etre*** of sculpture and its choice of the human form as its material. But the character saves it from this category; what one may almost call its psychological interest redeems its superficial triviality.

M. Saint-Marceaux is always successful in this way. One has only to look at the eyes of his figures to be convinced how subtle is his art of expressing character. Here he swings quite clear of all convention and manifests his genius positively and directly. The unfathomable secret of the tomb is in the spiritual expression of the guarding genius, and the elaborately complex movement concentrated upon the urn and directly inspired by the ephebes of the Sistine ceiling is a mere blind. The same is true of the portrait heads which within his range M. Saint Marceaux does better than almost anyone. M. Renan's "Confessions" hardly convey as distinct a notion of character as his bust exhibited at the Triennial of 1883. Many of the sculptors' anonymous heads, so to speak, are hardly less remarkable. Long after the sharp edge of one's interest in the striking pose of his "Harlequin" and the fine movement and bizarre features of his "Genius" has worn away, their curious spiritual interest, the individual *cachet* of their character, will sustain them. And so integrally true is this of all the productions of M. Saint-Marceaux's talent, that it is quite as perceptible in works where it is not accentuated and emphasized as it is in those of which I have been speaking; it is a quality that will bear refining, that is even better indeed in its more subtle manifestations. The figure of the Luxembourg Gallery, the young Dante reading Virgil, is an example; a girl's head, the forehead swathed in a turban, first exhibited some years ago, is another. The charm of these is more penetrating, though they are by no means either as popular or as "important" works as the "Genius of the Tomb" or the "Harlequin." In the time to come M. Saint-Marceaux will probably rely more and more on their quality of grave and yet alert distinction, and less on striking and eccentric variations of themes from Michael Angelo like the "Genius," and illustrations like the "Harlequin" of the artistic potentialities of the Canova sculpture.

With considerably less force than M. Dubois and decidedly less piquancy than M. Saint-Marceaux, M. Antonin Mercie has perhaps greater refinement than either. His outline is a trifle softer, his sentiment more gracious, more suave. His work is difficult to characterize satisfactorily, and the fact may of course proceed from its lack of force, as well as from the well-understood difficulty of translating into epithets anything so essentially elusive as suavity and grace of form. At one epoch in any examination of academic French sculpture that of M. Mercie seems the most interesting; it is so free from exaggeration of any kind on the one hand, it realizes its idea so satisfactorily on the other, and this idea is so agreeable, so refined, and at the same time so dignified. The "David" is an early work now in the Luxembourg gallery, reproductions of which are very popular, and the reader may judge how well it justifies these remarks. Being an early work, one cannot perhaps insist on its originality; in France, a young sculptor must be original at his peril; his education is so complete, he must have known and studied the beauties of classic sculpture so thoroughly, that not to be impressed by them so profoundly as to display his appreciativeness in his first work is apt to argue a certain insensitiveness. And every one cannot have creative genius. What a number of admirable works we should be compelled to forego if creative genius were demanded of an artist of the present day when the best minds of the time are occupied with other things than art! One is apt to forget that in our day the minds that correspond with the artistic miracles of the Renaissance are absorbed in quite different departments of effort. M. Mercie's "David" would perhaps never have existed but for Donatello's. As far as plastic motive is concerned, it may without injustice be called a variant of that admirable creation, and from every point of view except that of dramatic grace it is markedly inferior to its inspiration; as an embodiment of triumphant youth, of the divine ease with which mere force is overcome, it has only a superficial resemblance to the original.

But if with M. Mercie "David" was simply a classic theme to be treated, which is exactly what it of course was not with Donatello, it is undeniable that he has expressed himself very distinctly in his treatment. A less sensitive artist would have vulgarized instead of merely varying the conception, whereas one can easily see in M. Mercie's handling of it the ease, science, and felicitous movement that have since expressed themselves more markedly, more positively, but hardly more unmistakably, in the sculptor's maturer works. Of these the chief is perhaps the "Gloria Victis," which now decorates the Square Montholon; and its identity of authorship with the "David" is apparent in spite of its structural complexity and its far greater importance both in subject and execution. Its subject is the most inspiring that a French sculptor since the events of 1870-71 (so lightly considered by those who only see the theatric side of French character) could treat. Its general interest, too, is hardly inferior; there is something generally ennobling in the celebration of the virtues of the brave defeated that surpasses the commonplace of paeans. M. Mercie was, in this sense, more fortunate than the sculptor to whom the Berlinese owe the bronze commemoration of their victory. Perhaps to call his treatment entirely worthy of the theme, is to forget the import of such works as the tombs of the Medici Chapel at Florence. There is a region into whose precincts the dramatic quality penetrates only to play an insufficient part. But in modern art to do more than merely to keep such truths in mind, to insist on satisfactory plastic illustrations of them, is not only to prepare disappointment for one's self, but to risk misjudging admirable and elevated effort; and to regret the fact that France had only M. Mercie and not Michael Angelo to celebrate her "Gloria Victis" is to commit both of these errors. After all, the subjects are different, and the events of 1870-71 had compensations for France which the downfall of Florentine liberty was without; so that, indeed, a note of unmixed melancholy, however lofty its strain, would have been a discord which M. Mercie has certainly avoided. He has avoided it in rather a marked way, it is true. His monument is dramatic and stirring rather than inwardly moving. It is rhetorical rather than truly poetic; and the admirable quality of its rhetoric, its complete freedom from vulgar or sentimental alloy--its immense superiority to Anglo-Saxon rhetoric, in fine--does not conceal the truth that it is rhetoric, that it is prose and not poetry after all. Mercie's "Gloria Victis" is very fine; I know nothing so fine in modern sculpture outside of France. But then there is not very much that is fine at all in modern sculpture outside of France; and modern French sculpture, and M. Mercie along with it as one of its most eminent ornaments, have made it impossible to speak of them in a relative way. The antique and the Renaissance sculpture alone furnish their fit association, and like the Renaissance and the antique sculpture they demand a positive and absolute, and not a comparative criticism.

V

Well, then, speaking thus absolutely and positively, the cardinal defect of the Institute sculpture--and the refined and distinguished work of M. Mercie better perhaps than almost any other assists us to see this--is its over-carefulness for style. This is indeed the explanation of what I mentioned at the outset as the chief characteristic of this sculpture, the academic inelasticity, namely, with which it essays to reproduce the Renaissance romanticism. But for the fondness for style integral in the French mind and character, it would perceive the contradiction between this romanticism and any canons except such as are purely intuitive and indefinable. In comparison with the Renaissance sculptors, the French academic sculptors of the present day are certainly too exclusive devotees of Buffon's "order and movement,"

and too little occupied with the thought itself--too little individual. In comparison
with the antique, this is less apparent, but I fancy not less real. We are so accustomed
to think of the antique as the pure and simple embodiment of style, as a sublima-
tion, so to speak of the individual into style itself, that in this respect we are scarcely
fair judges of the antique. In any case we know very little of it; we can hardly speak
of it except by periods. But it is plain that the Greek is so superior to any subsequent
sculpture in this one respect of style that we rarely think of its other qualities. Our
judgment is inevitably a comparative one, and inevitably a comparative judgment
fixes our attention on the Greek supremacy of style. Indeed, in looking at the antique the thought itself is often alien to us, and the order and movement, being
more nearly universal perhaps, are all that occupy us. A family tombstone lying in
the cemetery at Athens, and half buried in the dust which blows from the Piraeus
roadway, has more style than M. Mercie's "Quand-Meme" group for Belfort, which
has been the subject of innumerable encomiums, and which has only style and no
individuality whatever to commend it. And the Athenian tombstone was probably furnished to order by the marble-cutting artist of the period, corresponding
to those whose signs one sees at the entrances of our own large cemeteries. Still
we may be sure that the ordinary Athenian citizen who adjudged prizes between
AEschylus and Sophocles, and to whom Pericles addressed the oration which only
exceptional culture nowadays thoroughly appreciates, found plenty of individuality
in the decoration of the Parthenon, and was perfectly conscious of the difference
between Phidias and his pupils. Even now, if one takes the pains to think of it, the
difference between such works as the so-called "Genius" of the Vatican and the
Athenian marbles, or between the Niobe group at Florence and the Venus torso
at Naples, for example, seems markedly individual enough, though the element of
style is still to our eyes the most prominent quality in each. Indeed, if one really
reflects upon the subject, it will not seem exaggeration to say that to anyone who
has studied both with any thoroughness it would be more difficult to individualize
the mass of modern French sculpture than even that of the best Greek epoch--the
epoch when style was most perfect, when its reign was, as it sometimes appears to
us, most absolute. And if we consider the Renaissance sculpture, its complexity is
so great, its individuality is so pronounced, that one is apt to lose sight of the important part which style really plays in it. In a work by Donatello we see first of all

his thought; in a Madonna of Mino's it is the idea that charms us; the Delia Robbia frieze at Pistoja is pure *genre*.

But modern academic French sculpture feels the weight of De Musset's handicap--it is born too late into a world too old. French art in general feels this, I think, and painting suffers from it equally with sculpture. Culture, the Institute, oppress individuality. But whereas Corot and Millet have triumphed over the Institute there are--there were, at least, till yesterday--hardly any Millets and Corots of sculpture whose triumph is as yet assured. The tendency, the weight of authority, the verdict of criticism, always conservative in France, are all the other way. At the Ecole des Beaux-Arts one learns, negatively, not to be ridiculous. This is a great deal; it is more than can be learned anywhere else nowadays--witness German, Italian, above all English exhibitions. Positively one learns the importance of style; and if it were not for academic French sculpture, one would say that this was something the importance of which could not be exaggerated. But in academic French sculpture it is exaggerated, and, what is fatal, one learns to exaggerate it in the schools. The traditions of Houdon are noticeably forgotten. Not that Houdon's art is not eminently characterized by style; the "San Bruno" at Rome is in point of style an antique. But compare his "Voltaire" in the foyer of the Comedie Francaise with Chapu's "Berryer" of the Palais de Justice, to take one of the very finest portrait-statues of the present day. Chapu's statue is more than irreproachable, it is elevated and noble, it is in the grand style; but it is plain that its impressiveness is due to the fact that the subject is conceived as the Orator in general and handled with almost a single eye to style. The personal interest that accentuates every detail of the "Voltaire"--the physiognomy, the pose, the right hand, are marvellously characteristic--simply is not sought for in Chapu's work. Of this quality there is more in Houdon's bust of Moliere, whom of course Houdon never saw, than in almost any production of the modern school. Chapu's works, and such exceptions as the heads of Baudry and Renan already mentioned, apart, one perceives that the modern school has made too many statues of the Republique, too many "Ledas" and "Susannahs" and "Quand-Memes" and "Gloria Victis." And its penchant for Renaissance canons only emphasizes the absolute commonplace of many of these.

On the other hand, if Houdon's felicitous harmony of style and individual force are forgotten, there is hardly any recognized succession to the imaginative freedom,

the *verve*, the triumphant personal fertility of Rude and Carpeaux. At least, such as
there is has not preserved the dignity and in many instances scarcely the decorum of
those splendid artists. Much of the sculpture which figures at the yearly Salons is, to
be sure, the absolute negation of style; its main characteristic is indeed eccentricity;
its main virtues, sincerity (which in art, of course, is only a very elementary virtue)
and good modelling (which in sculpture is equally elementary). Occasionally in the
midst of this display of fantasticality there is a work of promise or even of positive
interest. The observer who has not a weak side for the graceful conceits, invariably
daintily presented and beautifully modelled, of M. Moreau-Vauthier for example,
must be hard to please; they are of the very essence of the *article de Paris*, and only
abnormal primness can refuse to recognize the truth that the *article de Paris* has
its art side. M. Moreau-Vauthier is not perhaps a modern Cellini; he has certainly
never produced anything that could be classed with the "Perseus" of the Loggia de'
Lanzi, or even with the Fontainebleau "Diana;" but he does more than anyone else
to keep alive the tradition of Florentine preciosity, and about everything he does
there is something delightful.

Still the fantastic has not made much headway in the Institute, and it is so foreign to the French genius, which never tolerates it after it has ceased to be novel,
that it probably never will. It is a great tribute to French "catholicity of mind and
largeness of temper" that Carpeaux's "La Danse" remains in its position on the facade of the Grand Opera. French sentiment regarding it was doubtless accurately
expressed by the fanatic who tried to ink it indelibly after it was first exposed. This
vandal was right from his point of view--the point of view of style. Almost the one
work of absolute spontaneity among the hundreds which without and within decorate M. Garnier's edifice, it is thus a distinct jar in the general harmony; it distinctly
mars the "order and movement" of M. Garnier's thought, which is fundamentally
opposed to spontaneity. But imagine the devotion to style of a *milieu* in which a
person who would throw ink on a confessedly fine work of art is actuated by an
impersonal dislike of incongruity! Dislike of the incongruous is almost a French
passion, and, like all qualities, it has its defect, the defect of tolerating the conventional. It is through this tolerance, for example, that one of the freest of French
critics of art, a true Voltairian, Stendhal, was led actually to find Guido's ideal of
beauty higher than Raphael's, and to miss entirely the grandeur of Tintoretto. Criti-

cal opinion in France has not changed radically since Stendhal's day.

VI

The French sculptor may draw his inspiration from the sources of originality itself, his audience will measure the result by conventions. It is this fact undoubtedly that is largely responsible for the over-carefulness for style already remarked. Hence the work of M. Aime-Millet and of Professors Guillaume and Cavelier, and the fact that they are professors. Hence also the election of M. Falguiere to succeed to the chair of the Beaux-Arts left vacant by the death of Jouffroy some years ago. All of these have done admirable work. Professor Guillaume's Gracchi group at the Luxembourg is alone enough to atone for a mass of productions of which the "Castalian Fount" of a recent Salon is the cold and correct representative. Cavalier's "Gluck," destined for the Opera, is spirited, even if a trifle galvanic. Millet's "Apollo," which crowns the main gable of the Opera, stands out among its author's other works as a miracle of grace and rhythmic movement. M. Falguiere's admirers, and they are numerous, will object to the association here made. Falguiere's range has always been a wide one, and everything he has done has undoubtedly merited a generous portion of the prodigious encomiums it has invariably obtained. Yet, estimating it in any other way than by energy, variety, and mass, it is impossible to praise it highly with precision. It is too plainly the work of an artist who can do one thing as well as another, and of which cleverness is, after all, the spiritual standard. Bartholdi, who also should not be forgotten in any sketch of French sculpture, would, I am sure, have acquitted himself more satisfactorily than Falguiere did in the colossal groups of the Trocadero and the Arc de Triomphe de l'Etoile. To acquit himself satisfactorily is Bartholdi's specialty. These two groups are the largest and most important that a sculptor can have to do. The crowning of the Arc de Triomphe at least was a splendid opportunity. Neither of them had any distinction of outline, of mass, of relation, or of idea. Both were conventional to the last degree. That on the Arc had even its ludicrous details, such as occur only from artistic absent-mindedness in a work conceived and executed in a fatigued and hackneyed spirit. The "Saint Vincent de Paul" of the Pantheon, which justly passes for the sculptor's ***chef-d'oeuvre*** is in idea a work of large humanity. M. Falguiere is behind no one in ability to conceive a subject of this kind with propriety, and his subject here is inspiring if ever a subject was. The "Petit Martyr" of the Luxembourg has a real charm, but it too is content with too little, as one finds out in seeing it often; and it is in no sense a large work, scarcely larger than the tiresomely popular "Running Boy" of the same museum, which nevertheless in its day marked an epoch in modelling. Indeed, so slight is the spiritual hold that M. Falguiere has on one, that it really seems as if he were at his best in such a frankly carnal production as his since variously modified "Nymph Hunting" of the Triennial Exposition of 1883. The idea is nothing or next to nothing, but the surface ***faire*** is superb.

M. Barrias, M. Delaplanche, and M. Le Feuvre have each of them quite as much spontaneity as M. Falguiere, though the work of neither is as important in mass and variety. M. Delaplanche is always satisfactory, and beyond this there is something large about what he does that confers dignity even in the absence of quick interest. His proportions are simple, his outline flowing, and the agreeable ease of his compositions makes up to a degree for any lack of sympathetic sentiment or impressive significance: witness his excellent "Maternal Instruction," of the little park in front of Sainte Clothilde. M. Le Feuvre's qualities are very nearly the reverse of these: he has a fondness for integrity quite hostile in his case to simplicity. In his very frank appeal to one's susceptibility he is a little careless of sculptural considerations, which he is prone to sacrifice to pictorial ends. The result is a mannerism that in the end ceases to impress, and even becomes disagreeable. As nearly as may be in a French sculptor it borders on sentimentality, and finally the swaying attitudes of his figures become limp, and the startled-fawn eyes of his maidens and youths appear less touching than lackadaisical. But his being himself too conscious of it should not obscure the fact that he has a way of his own. M. Barrias is an artist of considerably greater powers than either M. Le Feuvre or M. Delaplanche; but one has a vague perception that his powers are limited, and that to desire in his case what one so sincerely wishes in the case of M. Dubois, namely, that he would "let himself go," would be unwise. Happily, when he is at his best there is no temptation to form such a wish. The "Premieres Funerailles" is a superb work--"the chef-d'oeuvre of our modern sculpture," a French critic enthusiastically terms it. It is hardly that; it has hardly enough spiritual distinction--not quite enough of either elegance or elevation--to merit such sweeping praise. But it may be justly termed, I think, the most completely representative of the masterpieces of that sculpture. Its triumph over the prodigious difficulties of elaborate composition "in the round"--difficulties to which M. Barrias succumbed in the "Spartacus" of the Tuileries Gardens--and its success in subordinating the details of a group to the end of enforcing a single motive, preserving the while their individual interest, are complete. Nothing superior in this respect has been done since John of Bologna's "Rape of the Sabines."

VII

M. Emmanuel Fremiet occupies a place by himself. There have been but two modern sculptors who have shown an equally pronounced genius for representing animals--namely, Barye, of course, and Barye's clever but not great pupil, Cain. The tigress in the Central Park, perhaps the best bronze there (the competition is not exacting), and the best also of the several variations of the theme of which, at one time, the sculptor apparently could not tire, familiarizes Americans with the talent of Cain. In this association Rouillard, whose horse in the Trocadero Gardens is an animated and elegant work, ought to be mentioned, but it is hardly as good as the neighboring elephant of Fremiet as mere animal representation (the *genre* exists and has excellences and defects of its own), while in more purely artistic worth it is quite eclipsed by its rival. Still if *fauna* is interesting in and of itself, which no one who knows Barye's work would controvert, it is still more interesting when, to put it brutally, something is done with it. In his ambitious and colossal work at the Trocadero, M. Fremiet does in fact use his *fauna* freely as artistic material, though at first sight it is its zooelogical interest that appears paramount. The same is true of the elephant near by, in which it seems as if he had designedly attacked the difficult problem of rendering embodied awkwardness decorative. Still more conspicuous, of course, is the artistic interest, the fancy, the humor, the sportive grace of his Luxembourg group of a young satyr feeding honey to a brace of bear's cubs, because he here concerns himself more directly with his idea and gives his genius freer play. And everyone will remember the sensation caused by his impressively repulsive "Gorilla Carrying off a Woman." But it is when he leaves this kind of thing entirely, and, wholly forgetful of his studies at the Jardin des Plantes, devotes himself to purely monumental work, that he is at his best. And in saying this I do not at all mean to insist on the superiority of monumental sculpture to the sculpture of *fauna*; it is superior, and Barye himself cannot make one content with the exclusive consecration of admirable talent to picturesque anatomy illustrating distinctly unintellectual passions. M. Fremiet, in ecstasy over his picturesque anatomy at the Jardin des Plantes, would scout this; but it is nevertheless true that in such works as the "Age de la pierre," which, if it may be called a monumental clock-top, is nevertheless certainly monumental; his "Louis d'Orleans," in the quadrangle of the restored Chateau de Pierrefonds; his "Jeanne d'Arc" (the later statue is not, I think, essentially different from the earlier one); and his "Torch-bearer" of the Middle Ages, in the new Hotel de Ville of Paris, not only is his subject a subject of loftier and more enduring interest than his elephants and deer and bears, but his own genius finds a more congenial medium of expression. In other words, any one who has seen his "Torch-bearer" or his "Louis d'Orleans" must conclude that M. Fremiet is losing his time at the Jardin des Plantes. In monumental works of the sort he displays a commanding dignity that borders closely upon the grand style itself. The "Jeanne d'Arc" is indeed criticised for lack of style. The horse is fine, as always with M. Fremiet; the action of both horse and rider is noble, and the homogeneity of the two, so to speak, is admirably achieved. But the character of the Maid is not perfectly satisfactory to *a priori* critics, to critics who have more or less hard and fast notions about the immiscibility of the heroic and the familiar. The "Jeanne d'Arc" is of course a heroic statue, illustrating one of the most puissant of profane legends; and it is unquestionably familiar and, if one chooses, defiantly unpretentious. Perhaps the Maid as M. Fremiet represents her could never have accomplished legend-producing deeds. Certainly she is the Maid neither of Chapu, nor of Bastien-Lepage, nor of the current convention. She is, rather, pretty, sympathetically childlike, *mignonne*; but M. Fremiet's conception is an original and a gracious one, and even the critic addicted to formulae has only to forget its title to become thoroughly in love with it; beside this merit *a priori* shortcomings count very little. But the other two works just mentioned are open to no objection of this kind or of any other, and in the category to which they belong they are splendid works. Since Donatello and Verrocchio nothing of the kind has been done which surpasses them; and it is only M. Fremiet's penchant for animal sculpture, and his fondness for exercising his lighter fancy in comparatively trivial *objets de vertu*, that obscure in any degree his fine talent for illustrating the grand style with natural ease and large simplicity.

VIII

I have already mentioned the most representative among those who have "arrived" of the school of academic French sculpture as it exists to-day, though it would be easy to extend the list with Antonin Carles, whose "Jeunesse" of the World's Fair of 1889 is a very graceful embodiment of adolescence; Suchetet, whose "Byblis" of the same exhibition caused his early death to be deplored; Adrien Gaudez, Etcheto, Idrac, and, of course, many others of distinction. There is no looseness in characterizing this as a "school;" it has its own qualities and its corresponding defects. It stands by itself--apart from the Greek sculpture and from its inspiration, the Renaissance, and from the more recent traditions of Houdon, or of Rude and Carpeaux. It is a thoroughly legitimate and unaffected expression of national thought and feeling at the present time, at once splendid and simple. The moment of triumph in any intellectual movement is, however, always a dangerous one. A slack-water period of intellectual slothfulness nearly always ensues. Ideas which have previously been struggling to get a hearing have become accepted ideas that have almost the force of axioms; no one thinks of their justification, of their basis in real truth and fact; they take their place in the great category of conventions. The mind feels no longer the exhilaration of discovery, the stimulus of fresh perception; the sense becomes jaded, enthusiasm impossible. Dealing with the same material and guided by the same principles, its production becomes inevitably hackneyed, artificial, lifeless; the *Zeit-Geist*, the Time-Spirit, is really a kind of Sisyphus, and the essence of life is movement. This law of perpetual renewal, of the periodical quickening of the human spirit, explains the barrenness of the inheritance of the greatest men; shows why originality is a necessary element of perfection; why Phidias, Praxiteles, Donatello, Michael Angelo (not to go outside of our subject), had no successors. Once a thing is done it is done for all time, and the study of perfection itself avails only as a stimulus to perfection in other combinations. In fact, the more nearly perfect the model the greater the necessity for an absolute break with it in order to secure anything like an equivalent in living force; in ***its*** direction at least everything vital has been done. So its lack of original force, its over-carefulness for style, its inevitable sensitiveness to the criticism that is based on convention, make the weak side of the French academic sculpture of the present day, fine and triumphant as it is. That the national thought and feeling are not a little conventional, and have the academic rather than a spontaneous inspiration, has, however, lately been distinctly felt as a misfortune and a limitation by a few sculptors whose work may be called the beginning of a new movement out of which, whatever may be its own limitations, nothing but good can come to French sculpture and of which the protagonists are Auguste Rodin and Jules Dalou.

VI

THE NEW MOVEMENT IN SCULPTURE
I

Side by side with the academic current in French art has moved of recent years a naturalist and romantic impulse whose manifestations have been always vigorous though occasionally exaggerated. In any of the great departments of activity nationally pursued--as art has been pursued in France since Francis I.--there are always these rival currents, of which now one and now the other constantly affects the ebb and flow of the tide of thought and feeling. The classic and romantic duel of 1830, the rise of the naturalist opposition to Hugo and romanticism in our own day, are familiar instances of this phenomenon in literature. The revolt of Gericault and Delacroix against David and Ingres are equally well known in the field of painting. Of recent years the foundation of the periodical *L'Art* and its rivalry with the conservative **Gazette des Beaux Arts** mark with the same definiteness, and an articulate precision, the same conflict between truth, as new eyes see it, and tradition. Never, perhaps, since the early Renaissance, however, has nature asserted her supremacy over convention in such unmistakable, such insistent, and, one may say, I think, such intolerant fashion as she is doing at the present moment. Sculpture, in virtue of the defiant palpability of its material, is the most impalpable of the plastic arts, and therefore it feels less quickly than the rest, perhaps, the impress of the influences of the epoch and their classifying canons. Natural imitation shows first in sculpture, and subsists in it longest. But convention once its conqueror, the return to nature is here most tardy, because, owing to the impalpable, the elusive quality of sculpture, though natural standards may everywhere else be in vogue, no one thinks of applying them to so specialized an expression. Its variation depends therefore more completely on the individual artist himself. Niccolo Pisano, for example, died when Giotto was two years old, but, at the other end of the historic line of modern art, it has taken years since Delacroix to furnish recognition for Auguste Rodin. The stronghold of the Institute had been mined many times by revolutionary painters before Dalou took the grand medal of the Salon.

Owing to the relative and in fact polemic position which these two artists occupy, the movement which they represent, and of which as yet they themselves form a chief part, a little obscures their respective personalities, which are nevertheless, in sculpture, by far the most positive and puissant of the present epoch. M. Rodin's work, especially, is so novel that one's first impression in its presence is of its implied criticism of the Institute. One thinks first of its attitude, its point of view, its end, aim, and means, and of the utter contrast of these with those of the accepted contemporary masters in his art--of Dubois and Chapu, Mercie and Saint-Marceaux. One judges generally, and instinctively avoids personal and direct impressions. The first thought is not, Are the "Saint Jean" and the "Bourgeois de Calais" successful works of art? But, *Can* they be successful if the accepted masterpieces of modern sculpture are not to be set down as insipid? One is a little bewildered. It is easy to see and to estimate the admirable traits and the shortcomings of M. Dubois's delightful and impressive reminiscences of the Renaissance, of M. Mercie's refined and graceful compositions. They are of their time and place. They embody, in distinguished manner and in an accentuated degree, the general inspiration. Their spiritual characteristics are traditional and universal, and technically, without perhaps often passing beyond it, they exhaust cleverness. You may enjoy or resent their classic and exemplary excellences, as you feel your taste to have suffered from the lack or the superabundance of academic influences; I cannot fancy an American insensitive to their charm. But it is plain that their perfection is a very different thing from the characteristics of a strenuous artistic personality seeking expression. If these latter when encountered are seen to be evidently of an extremely high order, contemporary criticism, at all events, should feel at once the wisdom of beginning with the endeavor to appreciate, instead of making the degree of its own familiarity with them the test of their merit.

French aesthetic authority, which did this in the instances of Barye, of Delacroix, of Millet, of Manet, of Puvis de Chavannes, did it also for many years in the instance of M. Rodin. It owes its defeat in the contest with him--for like the recalcitrants in the other contests, M. Rodin has definitively triumphed--to the unwise attempt to define him in terms heretofore applicable enough to sculptors, but wholly inapplicable to him. It failed to see that the thing to define in his work was the man himself, his temperament, his genius. Taken by themselves and considered as characteristics of the Institute sculptors, the obvious traits of this work might, that is to say, be adjudged eccentric and empty. Fancy Professor Guillaume suddenly subordinating academic disposition of line and mass to true structural expression! One would simply feel the loss of his accustomed style and harmony. With M. Rodin, who deals with nature directly, through the immediate force of his own powerful temperament, to feel the absence of the Institute training and traditions is absurd. The question in his case is simply whether or no he is a great artistic personality, an extraordinary and powerful temperament, or whether he is merely a turbulent and capricious protestant against the measure and taste of the Institute. But this is really no longer a question, however it may have been a few years ago; and when his Dante portal for the new Palais des Arts Decoratifs shall have been finished, and the public had an opportunity to see what the sculptor's friend and only serious rival, M. Dalou, calls "one of the most, if not the most original and astonishing pieces of sculpture of the nineteenth century," it will be recognized that M. Rodin, so far from being amenable to the current canon, has brought the canon itself to judgment.

How and why, people will perceive in proportion to their receptivity. Candor and intelligence will suffice to appreciate that the secret of M. Rodin's art is structural expression, and that it is this and not any superficial eccentricity of execution that definitely distinguishes him from the Institute. Just as his imagination, his temperament, his spiritual energy and ardor individualize the positive originality of his motive, so the expressiveness of his treatment sets him aside from all as well as from each of the Institute sculptors in what may be broadly called technical attitude. No sculptor has ever carried expression further. The sculpture of the present day has certainly not occupied itself much with it. The Institute is perhaps a little afraid of it. It abhors the *baroque* rightly enough, but very likely it fails to see that the expression of such sculpture as M. Rodin's no more resembles the contortions of the Dresden Museum giants than it does the composure of M. Delaplanche. The *baroque* is only violent instead of placid commonplace, and is as conventional as any professor of sculpture could desire. Expression means individual character completely exhibited rather than conventionally suggested. It is certainly not too much to say that in the sculpture of the present day the sense of individual character is conveyed mainly by convention. The physiognomy has usurped the place of the physique, the gesture of the form, the pose of the substance. And face, gesture, form are, when they are not brutally naturalistic and so not art at all, not individual and native, but typical and classic. Very much of the best modern sculpture might really have been treated like those antique figurines of which the bodies were made by wholesale, being supplied with individual heads when the time came for using them.

This has been measurably true since the disappearance of the classic dress and the concealment of the body by modern costume. The nudes of the early Renaissance, in painting still more than in sculpture, are differentiated by the faces. The rest of the figure is generally conventionalized as thoroughly as the face itself is in Byzantine and the hands in Giottesque painting. Giotto could draw admirably, it need not be said. He did draw as well as the contemporary feeling for the human figure demanded. When the Renaissance reached its climax and the study of the antique led artists to look beneath drapery and interest themselves in the form, expression made an immense step forward. Color was indeed almost lost sight of in the new interest, not to reappear till the Venetians. But owing to the lack of visible nudity, to the lack of the classic gymnasia, to the concealments of modern attire, the knowledge of and interest in the form remained, within certain limits, an esoteric affair. The general feeling, even where, as in the Italy of the *quattro* and *cinque centi*, everyone was a connoisseur, did not hold the artist to expression in his anatomy as the general Greek feeling did. Everyone was a connoisseur of art alone, not of nature as well. Consequently, in spite of such an enthusiastic genius as Donatello, who probably more than any other modern has most nearly approached the Greeks--not in spiritual attitude, for he was eminently of his time, but in his attitude toward nature--the human form in art has for the most part remained, not conventionalized as in the Byzantine and Gothic times, but thoroughly conventional. Michael Angelo himself certainly may be charged with lending the immense weight of his majestic genius to perpetuate the conventional. It is not his distortion of nature, as pre-Raphaelite limitedness glibly asserts, but his carelessness of her prodigious potentialities, that marks one side of his colossal accomplishment. Just as the lover of architecture as architecture will protest that Michael Angelo's was meretricious, however inspiring, so M. Rodin declares his sculpture unsatisfactory, however poetically impressive. "He used to do a little anatomy evenings," he said to me, "and used his chisel next day without a model. He repeats endlessly his one type--the youth of the Sistine ceiling. Any particular felicity of expression you are apt to find him borrowing from Donatello--such as, for instance, the movement of the arm of the 'David,' which is borrowed from Donatello's 'St. John Baptist.'" Most people to whom Michael Angelo's creations appear celestial in their majesty at once and in their winningness would deny this. But it is worth citing both because M. Rodin strikes so many crude apprehensions as a French Michael Angelo, whereas he is so radically removed from him in point of view and in practice that the unquestionable spiritual analogy between them is rather like that between kindred spirits working in different arts, and because, also, it shows not only what M. Rodin is not, but what he is. The grandiose does not run away with him. His imagination is occupied largely in following out nature's suggestions. His sentiment does not so drench and saturate his work as to float it bodily out of the realm of natural into that of supernal beauty, there to crystallize in decorative and puissant visions appearing out of the void and only superficially related to their corresponding natural forms. Standing before the Medicean tombs the modern susceptibility receives perhaps the most poignant, one may almost say the most intolerable, impression to be obtained from any plastic work by the hand of man; but it is a totally different impression from that left by the sculptures of the Parthenon pediments, not only because the sentiment is wholly different, but because in the great Florentine's work it is so overwhelming as wholly to dominate purely natural expression, natural character, natural beauty. In the Medici Chapel the soul is exalted; in the British Museum the mind is enraptured. The object itself seems to disappear in the one case, and to reveal itself in the other.

I do not mean to compare M. Rodin with the Greeks--from whom in sentiment and imagination he is, of course, as totally removed as what is intensely modern must be from the antique--any more than I mean to contrast him with Michael Angelo, except for the purposes of clearer understanding of his general aesthetic attitude. Association of anything contemporary with what is classic, and especially with what is greatest in the classic, is always a perilous proceeding. Very little time is apt to play havoc with such classification. I mean only to indicate that the resemblance to Michael Angelo, found by so many persons in such works as the Dante doors, is only of the loosest kind--as one might, through their common lusciousness, compare peaches with pomegranates--and that to the discerning eye, or the eye at all experienced in observing sculpture, M. Rodin's sculpture is far more closely related to that of Donatello and the Greeks. It, too, reveals rather than constructs beauty, and by the expression of character rather than by the suggestion of sentiment.

An illustration of M. Rodin's affinity with the antique is an incident which he related to me of his work upon his superb "Age d'Airain." He was in Naples; he saw nature in freer inadvertence than she allows elsewhere; he had the best of models. Under these favoring circumstances he spent three months on a leg of his statue; "which is equivalent to saying that I had at last absolutely mastered it," said he. One day in the Museo Nazionale he noticed in an antique the result of all his study and research. Nature, in other words, is M. Rodin's *material* in the same special sense in which it was the antique material, and in which, since Michael Angelo and the high Renaissance, it has been for the most part only the sculptor's *means*. It need not be said that the personality of the artist may be as strenuous in the one case as in the other; unless, indeed, we maintain, as perhaps we may, that individuality is more apt to atrophy in the latter instance; for as one gets farther and farther away from nature he is in more danger from conventionality than from caprice. And this is in fact what has happened since the high Renaissance, the long line of conventionalities being continued, sometimes punctuated here and there as by Clodion or Houdon, David, Rude, or Barye, sometimes rising into great dignity and refinement of style and intelligence, as in the contemporary sculpture of the Institute, but in general almost purely decorative or sentimental, and, so far as natural expression is concerned, confining itself to psychological rather than physical character.

What is it, for instance, that distinguishes a group like M. Dubois's "Charity" from the *genre* sentiment or incident of some German or Italian "professor?" Qualities of style, of refined taste, of elegance, of true intelligence. Its artistic interest is purely decorative and sentimental. Really what its average admirer sees in it is the same moral appeal that delights the simple admirers of German or Italian treatment of a similar theme. It is simply infinitely higher bred. Its character is developed no further. Its significance as form is not insisted on. The parts are not impressively differentiated, and their mysterious mutual relations and correspondences are not dwelt on. The physical character, with its beauties, its salient traits of every kind, appealing so strongly to the sculptor to whom nature appears plastic as well as suggestive, is wholly neglected in favor of the psychological suggestion. And the individual character, the *cachet* of the whole, the artistic essence and *ensemble*, that is to say, M. Dubois has, after the manner of most modern sculpture, conveyed in a language of convention, which since the time of the Siennese fountain, at all events, has been classical.

The literary artist does not proceed in this way. He does not content himself with telling us, for example, that one of his characters is a good man or a bad man, an able, a selfish, a tall, a blonde, or a stupid man, as the case may be. He takes every means to express his character, and to do it, according to M. Taine's definition of a work of art, more completely than it appears in nature. He recognizes its complexity and enforces the sense of reality by a thousand expedients of what one may almost call contrasting masses, derivative movements, and balancing planes. He distinguishes every possible detail that plays any structural part, and, in short, instead of giving us the mere symbol of the Sunday-school books, shows us a concrete organism at once characteristic and complex. Judged with this strictness, which in literary art is elementary, how much of the best modern sculpture is abstract, symbolic, purely typical. What insipid fragments most of the really eminent Institute statues would make were their heads knocked off by some band of modern barbarian invaders. In the event of such an irruption, would there be any torsos left from which future Poussins could learn all they should know of the human form? Would there be any *disjecta membra* from which skilled anatomists could reconstruct the lost *ensemble*, or at any rate make a shrewd guess at it? Would anything survive mutilation with the serene confidence in its fragmentary but everywhere penetrating interest which seems to pervade the most fractured fraction of a Greek relief on the Athenian acropolis? Yes, there would be the debris of Auguste Rodin's sculpture.

In our day the human figure has never been so well understood. Back of such expressive modelling as we note in the "Saint Jean," in the "Adam" and "Eve," in the "Calaisiens," in a dozen figures of the Dante doors, is a knowledge of anatomy such as even in the purely scientific profession of surgery can proceed only from an immense fondness for nature, an insatiable curiosity as to her secrets, an inexhaustible delight in her manifestations. From the point of view of such knowledge and such handling of it, it is no wonder that the representations of nature which issue from the Institute seem superficial. One can understand that from this point of view very delightful sculpture, very refined, very graceful, very perfectly understood within its limits, may appear like *baudruche*--inflated gold-beater's skin, that is to say, of which toy animals are made in France, and which has thus passed into studio *argot* as the figure for whatever lacks structure and substance. Ask M. Rodin the explanation of a movement, an attitude, in one of his works which strikes your convention-steeped sense as strange, and he will account for it just as an anatomical demonstrator would--pointing out its necessary derivation from some disposition of another part of the figure, and not at all dwelling on its grace or its other purely decorative felicity. Its artistic function in his eyes is to aid in expressing fully and completely the whole of which it forms a part, not to constitute a harmonious detail merely agreeable to the easily satisfied eye. But then the whole will look anatomical rather than artistic. There is the point exactly. Will it? I remember speculating about this in conversation with M. Rodin himself. "Isn't there danger," I said, "of getting too fond of nature, of dissecting with so much enthusiasm that the pleasure of discovery may obscure one's feeling for pure beauty, of losing the artistic in the purely scientific interest, of becoming pedantic, of imitating rather than constructing, of missing art in avoiding the artificial?" I had some difficulty in making myself understood; this perpetual see-saw of nature and art which enshrouds aesthetic dialectics as in a Scotch mist seems curiously factitious to the truly imaginative mind. But I shall always remember his reply, when he finally made me out, as one of the finest severings conceivable of a Gordian knot of this kind. "Oh, yes," said he; "there is, no doubt, such a danger for a mediocre artist."

M. Rodin is, whatever one may think of him, certainly not a mediocre artist. The instinct of self-preservation may incline the Institute to assert that he obtrudes his anatomy. But prejudice itself can blind no one of intelligence to his immense imaginative power, to his poetic "possession." His work precisely illustrates what I take to have been, at the best epochs, the relations of nature to such art as is loosely to be called imitative art--what assuredly were those relations in the mind of the Greek artist. Nature supplies the parts and suggests their cardinal relations. Insufficient study of her leaves these superficial and insipid. Inartistic absorption in her leaves them lifeless. The imagination which has itself conceived the whole, the idea, fuses them in its own heat into a new creation which is "imitative" only in the sense that its elements are not inventions. The art of sculpture has retraced its steps far enough to make pure invention, as of Gothic griffins and Romanesque symbology, unsatisfactory to everyone. But, save in M. Rodin's sculpture, it has not fully renewed the old alliance with nature on the old terms--Donatello's terms; the terms which exact the most tribute from nature, which insist on her according her completest significance, her closest secrets, her faculty of expressing character as well as of suggesting sentiment. Very beautiful works are produced without her aid to this extent. We may be sure of this without asking M. Rodin to admit it. He would not do his own work so well were he prepared to; as Millet pointed out when asked to write a criticism of some other painter's canvas, in estimating the production of his fellows an artist is inevitably handicapped by the feeling that he would have done it very differently himself. It is easy not to share M. Rodin's gloomy vaticinations as to French sculpture based on the continued triumph of the Institute style and suavity. The Institute sculpture is too good for anyone not himself engaged in the struggle to avoid being impressed chiefly by its qualities to the neglect of its defects. At the same time it is clear that no art can long survive in undiminished vigor that does not from time to time renew its vitality by resteeping itself in the influences of nature. And so M. Rodin's service to French sculpture becomes, at the present moment, especially signal and salutary because French sculpture, however refined and delightful, shows, just now, very plainly the tendency toward the conventional which has always proved so dangerous, and because M. Rodin's work is a conspicuous, a shining example of the return to nature on the part not of a mere realist, naturalist, or other variety of "mediocre artist," but of a profoundly poetic and imaginative temperament.

This is why, one immediately perceives in studying his works, Rodin's treatment, while exhausting every contributary detail to the end of complete expression, is never permitted to fritter away its energy either in the mystifications of optical illusion, or in the infantine idealization of what is essentially subordinate and ancillary. This is why he devotes three months to the study of a leg, for example--not to copy, but to "possess" it. Indeed, no sculptor of our time has made such a sincere and, in general, successful, effort to sink the sense of the material in the conception, the actual object in the artistic idea. One loses all sense of bronze or marble, as the case may be, not only because the artistic significance is so overmastering that one is exclusively occupied in apprehending it, but because there are none of those superficial graces, those felicities of surface modelling, which, however they may delight, infallibly distract as well. Such excellences have assuredly their place. When the motive is conventional or otherwise insipid, or even when its character is distinctly light without being trivial, they are legitimately enough agreeable. And because, in our day, sculptural motives have generally been of this order we have become accustomed to look for such excellences, and, very justly, to miss them when they are absent. Grace of pose, suavity of outline, pleasing disposition of mass, smooth, round deltoids and osseous articulations, and perpetually changing planes of flesh and free play of muscular movement, are excellences which, in the best of academic French sculpture, are sensuously delightful in a high degree. But they invariably rivet our attention on the successful way in which the sculptor has used his bronze or marble to decorative ends, and when they are accentuated so as to dominate the idea they invariably enfeeble its expression. With M. Rodin one does not think of his material at all; one does not reflect whether he used it well or ill, caused it to lose weight and immobility to the eye or not, because all his superficial modelling appears as an inevitable deduction from the way in which he has conceived his larger subject, and not as "handling" at all. In reality, of course, it is the acme of sensitive handling. The point is a nice one. His practice is a dangerous one. It would be fatal to a less strenuous temperament. To leave, in a manner and so far as obvious insistence on it goes, "handling" to take care of itself, is to incur the peril of careless, clumsy, and even brutal, modelling, which, so far from dissembling its existence behind the prominence of the idea, really emphasizes itself unduly because of its imperfect and undeveloped character. Detail that is neglected really acquires a greater prominence than detail that is carried too far, because it is sensuously disagreeable.

But when an artist like M. Rodin conceives his spiritual subject so largely and with so much intensity that mere sensuous agreeableness seems too insignificant to him even to be treated with contempt, he treats his detail solely with reference to its centripetal and organic value, which immediately becomes immensely enhanced, and the detail itself, dropping thus into its proper place, takes on a beauty wholly transcending the ordinary agreeable aspect of sculptural detail. And the *ensemble*, of course, is in this way enforced as it can be in no other, and we get an idea of Victor Hugo or St. John Baptist so powerfully and yet so subtly suggested, that the abstraction seems actually all that we see in looking at the concrete bust or statue. Objections to M. Rodin's "handling" as eccentric or capricious, appear to the sympathetic beholder of one of his majestic works the very acme of misappreciation, and their real excuse--which is, as I have said, the fact that such "handling" is as unfamiliar as the motives it accompanies--singularly poor and feeble.

As for the common nature of these motives, the character of the personality which appears in their varied presentments, it is almost idle to speak in the absence of the work itself, so eloquent is this at once and so untranslatable. But it may be said approximately that M. Rodin's temperament is in the first place deeply romantic. Everything the Institute likes repels him. He has the poetic conception of art and its mission, and in poetry any authoritative and codifying consensus seems to him paradoxical. Style, in his view, unless it is something wholly uncharacterizable, is a vague and impalpable spirit breathing through the work of some strongly marked individuality, or else it is formalism. He delights in the fantasticality of the Gothic. The west facade of Rouen inspires him more than all the formulae of Palladian proportions. He detests systematization. He reads Shakespeare, Schiller, Dante almost exclusively. He sees visions and dreams dreams. The awful in the natural forces, moral and material, seems his element. He believes in freedom, in the absolute emancipation of every faculty. As for study, study nature. If then you fail in restraint and measure you are a "mediocre artist," whom no artificial system devised to secure measure and restraint could have rescued from essential insignificance. No poet or landscape painter ever delighted more in the infinitely varied suggestiveness and exuberance of nature, or ever felt the formality of much that passes for art as more chill and drear. Hence in all his works we have the sense, first of all, of an overmastering sincerity; then of a prodigious wealth of fancy; then of a marvellous

acquaintance with his material. His imagination has all the vivacity and tumultu-
ousness of Rubens's, but its images, if not better understood, which would perhaps
be impossible, are more compact and their evolution more orderly. And they are
furthermore one and all vivified by a wholly remarkable feeling for beauty. In spite
of all his knowledge of the external world, no artist of our time is more completely
mastered by sentiment. In the very circumstance of being free from such conventions as the cameo relief, the picturesque costume details, the goldsmith's work
characteristic of the Renaissance, now so much in vogue, M. Rodin's things acquire
a certain largeness and loftiness as well as simplicity and sincerity of sentiment. The
same model posed for the "Saint Jean" that posed for a dozen things turned out of
the academic studios, but compared with the result in the latter cases, that in the
former is even more remarkable for sentiment than for its structural sapience and
general physical interest. How perfectly insignificant beside its moral impressiveness are the graceful works whose sentiment does not result from the expression of
the form, but is conveyed in some convention of pose, of gesture, of physiognomy!
It is like the contrast between a great and a graceful actor. The one interests you by
his intelligent mastery of convention, by the tact and taste with which he employs
in voice, carriage, facial expression, gesture, diction, the several conventions according to which ideas and emotions are habitually conveyed to your comprehension.
Salvini, Coquelin, Got, pass immediately outside the realm of conventions. Their
language, their medium of communication, is as new as what it expresses. They are
inventive as well as intelligent. Their effect is prodigiously heightened because in
this way, the warp as well as the woof of their art being expressive and original, the
artistic result is greatly fortified. Given the same model, M. Rodin's result is in like
manner expressly and originally enforced far beyond the result toward which the
academic French school employs the labels of the Renaissance as conventionally as
its predecessor at the beginning of the century employed those of the antique. "Formerly we used to do Greek," says M. Rodin, with no small justice; "now we do Italian. That is all the difference there is." And I cannot better conclude this imperfect
notice of the work of a great master, in characterizing which such epithets as majestic, Miltonic, grandiose suggest themselves first of all, than by calling attention
to the range which it covers, and to the fact that, even into the domain which one
would have called consecrate to the imitators of the antique and the Renaissance,

M. Rodin's informing sentiment and sense of beauty penetrate with their habitual distinction; and that the little child's head entitled "Alsace," that considerable portion of his work represented by "The Wave and the Shore," for example, and a small ideal female figure, which the manufacturer might covet for reproduction, but which, as Bastien-Lepage said to me, is "a definition of the essence of art," are really as noble as his more majestic works are beautiful.

II

Aube is another sculptor of acknowledged eminence who ranges himself with M. Rodin in his opposition to the Institute. His figures of "Bailly" and "Dante" are very fine, full of a most impressive dignity in the *ensemble*, and marked by the most vigorous kind of modelling. One may easily like his "Gambetta" less. But for years Rodin's only eminent fellow sculptor was Dalou. Perhaps his protestantism has been less pronounced than M. Rodin's. It was certainly long more successful in winning both the connoisseur and the public. The state itself, which is now and then even more conservative than the Institute, has charged him with important works, and the Salon has given him its highest medal. And he was thus recognized long before M. Rodin's works had risen out of the turmoil of critical contention to their present envied if not cordially approved eminence. But for being less energetic, less absorbed, less intense than M. Rodin's, M. Dalou's enthusiasm for nature involves a scarcely less uncompromising dislike of convention. He had no success at the Ecole des Beaux Arts. Unlike Rodin, he entered those precincts and worked long within them, but never sympathetically or felicitously. The rigor of academic precept was from the first excessively distasteful to his essentially and eminently romantic nature. He chafed incessantly. The training doubtless stood him in good stead when he found himself driven by hard necessity into commercial sculpture, into that class of work which is on a very high plane for its kind in Paris, but for which the manufacturer rather than the designer receives the credit. But he probably felt no gratitude to it for this, persuaded that but for its despotic prevalence there would have been a clearer field for his spontaneous and agreeable effort to win distinction in. He greatly preferred at this time the artistic anarchy of England, whither he betook himself after the Commune--not altogether upon compulsion, but by prudence perhaps; for like Rodin, his birth, his training, his disposition, his ideas, have always been as liberal and popular in politics as in art, and in France a man of any sincerity and dignity of character has profound political convictions, even though his profession be purely aesthetic. In England he was very successful both at the Academy and with the amateurs of the aristocracy, of many of whom he made portraits, besides finding ready purchasers among them for his imaginative works. The list of these latter begins, if we except some delightful decoration for one of the Champs-Elysees palaces, with a statue called "La Brodeuse," which won for him a medal at the Salon of 1870. Since then his production has been prodigious in view of its originality, of its lack of the powerful momentum extraneously supplied to the productive force that follows convention and keeps in the beaten track.

His numerous peasant subjects at one time led to comparison of him with Millet, but the likeness is of the most superficial kind. There is no spiritual kinship whatever between him and Millet. Dalou models the Marquis de Dreux-Breze with as much zest as he does his "Boulonnaise allaitant son enfant;" his touch is as sympathetic in his Rubens-like "Silenus" as in his naturalistic "Berceuse." Furthermore, there is absolutely no note of melancholy in his realism--which, at the present time, is a point well worth noting. His vivacity excludes the pathetic. Traces of Carpeaux's influence are plain in his way of conceiving such subjects as Carpeaux would have handled. No one could have come so closely into contact with that vigorous individuality without in some degree undergoing its impress, without learning to look for the alert and elegant aspects of his model, whatever it might be. But with Carpeaux's distinction Dalou has more poise. He is considerably farther away from the rococo. His ideal is equally to be summarized in the word Life, but he cares more for its essence, so to speak, than for its phenomena, or at all events manages to make it felt rather than seen. One perceives that humanity interests him on the moral side, that he is interested in its significance as well as its form. Accordingly with him the movement illustrates the form, which is in its turn truly expressive, whereas occasionally, so bitter was his disgust with the pedantry of the schools, with Carpeaux the form is used to exhibit movement. Then, too, M. Dalou has a certain nobility which Carpeaux's vivacity is a shade too animated to reach. Motive and treatment blend in a larger sweep. The graver substance follows the planes and lines of a statelier if less brilliant style. It **has**, in a word, more style.

I can find no exacter epithet, on the whole, for Dalou's large distinction, and conscious yet sober freedom, than the word Venetian. There is some subtle phrenotype that associates him with the great colorists. His work is, in fact, full of color, if one may trench on the jargon of the studios. It has the sumptuousness of Titian and Paul Veronese. Its motives are cast in the same ample mould. Many of his figures breathe the same air of high-born ease and well-being, of serene and not too intellectual composure. There is an aristocratic tincture even in his peasants--a kind of native distinction inseparable from his touch. And in his women there is a certain gracious sweetness, a certain exquisite and elusive refinement elsewhere caught only by Tintoretto, but illustrated by Tintoretto with such penetrating intensity as to leave perhaps the most nearly indelible impression that the sensitive amateur carries away with him from Venice. The female figures in the colossal group which should have been placed in the Place de la Republique, but was relegated by official stupidity to the Place des Nations, are examples of this patrician charm in carriage, in form, in feature, in expression. They have not the witchery, the touch of Bohemian sprightliness that make such figures as Carpeaux's "Flora" so enchanting, but they are at once sweeter and more distinguished. The sense for the exquisite which this betrays excludes all dross from M. Dalou's rich magnificence. Even the "Silenus" group illustrates exuberance without excess: I spoke of it just now as Rubenslike, but it is only because it recalls Rubens's superb strength and riotous fancy; it is in reality a Rubens-like motive purged in the execution of all Flemish grossness. There is even in Dalou's fantasticality of this sort a measure and distinction which temper animation into resemblance to such delicate blitheness as is illustrated by the Bargello "Bacchus" of Jacopo Sansovino. Sansovino afterward, by the way, amid the artificiality of Venice, whither he went, wholly lost his individual force, as M. Dalou, owing to his love of nature, is less likely to do. But his sketch for a monument to Victor Hugo, and perhaps still more his memorial of Delacroix in the Luxembourg Gardens, point warningly in this direction, and it would perhaps be easier than he supposes to permit his extraordinary decorative facility to lead him on to execute works unpenetrated by personal feeling, and recalling less the acme of the Renaissance than the period just afterward, when original effort had exhausted itself and the movement of art was due mainly to momentum--when, as in France at the present moment, the enormous mass of artistic production really forced pedantry upon culture, and prevented any but the most strenuous personalities from being genuine, because of the immensely increased authoritativeness of what had become classic.

Certainly M. Dalou is far more nearly in the current of contemporary art than his friend Rodin, who stands with his master Barye rather defiantly apart from the regular evolution of French sculpture, whereas one can easily trace the derivation of M. Dalou and his relations to the present and the immediate past of his art in his country. His work certainly has its Fragonard, its Clodion, its Carpeaux side. Like every temperament that is strongly attracted by the decorative as well as the significant and the expressive, pure style in and for itself has its fascinations, its temptations for him. Of course it does not succeed in getting the complete possession of him that it has of the Institute. And there is, as I have suggested, an important difference, disclosed in the fact that M. Dalou uses his faculty for style in a personal rather than in the conventional way. His decoration is distinctly Dalou, and not arrangements after classic formulae. It is full of zest, of ardor, of audacity. So that if his work has what one may call its national side, it is because the author's temperament is thoroughly national at bottom, and not because this temperament is feeble or has been academically repressed. But the manifest fitness with which it takes its place in the category of French sculpture shows the moral difference between it and the work of M. Rodin. Morally speaking, it is mainly--not altogether, but mainly--rhetorical, whereas M. Rodin's is distinctly poetic. It is delightful rhetoric and it has many poetic strains--such as the charm of penetrating distinction I have mentioned. But with the passions in their simplest and last analysis he hardly occupies himself at all. Such a work as "La Republique," the magnificent bas-relief of the Hotel de Ville in Paris, is a triumph of allegorical rhetoric, very noble, not a little moving, prodigious in its wealth of imaginative material, composed from the centre and not arranged with artificial felicity, full of suggestiveness, full of power, abounding in definite sculptural qualities, both moral and technical; it again is Rubens-like in its exuberance, but of firmer texture, more closely condensed. But anything approaching the ***kind*** of impressiveness of the Dante portal it certainly does not essay. It is in quite a different sphere. Its exaltation is, if not deliberate, admirably self-possessed. To find it theatrical would be simply a mark of our absurd Anglo-Saxon preference for reserve and repression in circumstances naturally suggesting expansion and elation--a preference surely born of timorousness and essentially very subtly theatrical itself. It is simply not deeply, intensely poetic, but, rather, a splendid piece of rhetoric, as I say.

So, too, is the famous Mirabeau relief, which is perhaps M. Dalou's masterpiece, and which represents his national side as completely as the group for the Place des Nations does those of his qualities I have endeavored to indicate by calling them Venetian. Observe the rare fidelity which has contributed its weight of sincerity to this admirable relief. Every prominent head of the many members of the Assembly, who nevertheless rally behind Mirabeau with a fine pell-mell freedom of artistic effect, is a portrait. The effect is like that of similar works designed and executed with the large leisure of an age very different from the competition and struggling hurry of our own. In every respect this work is as French as it is individual. It is penetrated with a sense of the dignity of French history. It is as far as possible re-moved from the cheap *genre* effect such a scheme in less skilful hands might easily have had. Mirabeau's gesture, in fact his entire presence, is superb, but the marquis is as fine in his way as the tribune in his. The beholder assists at the climax of a great crisis, unfolded to him in the impartial spirit of true art, quite without partisanship, and though manifestly stimulated by sympathy with the nobler cause, even more acutely conscious of the grandeur of the struggle and the distinction of those on all sides engaged in it, and acquiring from these a kind of elation, of exaltation such as the Frenchman experiences only when he may give expression to his artistic and his patriotic instincts at the same moment.

The distinctly national qualities of this masterpiece, and their harmonious as-sociation with the individual characteristics of M. Dalou, his love of nature, his native distinction, his charm, and his power, in themselves bear eminent witness to the vitality of modern French sculpture, in spite of all the influences which tend to petrify it with system and convention. M. Rodin stands so wholly apart that it would be unsafe perhaps to argue confidently from his impressive works the po-tentiality of periodical renewal in an art over which the Institute presides with still so little challenge of its title. But it is different with M. Dalou. Extraordinary as his talent is, its unquestioned and universal recognition is probably in great measure due to the preparedness of the environment to appreciate extraordinary work of the kind, to the high degree which French popular aesthetic education, in a word, has reached. And one's last word about contemporary French sculpture--even in closing a consideration of the works of such protestants as Rodin and Dalou--must be a recognition of the immense service of the Institute in education of this kind. Let some country without an institute, around which what aesthetic feeling the age permits may crystallize, however sharply, give us a Rodin and a Dalou!

The Codes Of Hammurabi And Moses
W. W. Davies

QTY

The discovery of the Hammurabi Code is one of the greatest achievements of archaeology, and is of paramount interest, not only to the student of the Bible, but also to all those interested in ancient history...

Religion   **ISBN:** *1-59462-338-4*   **Pages:132**

MSRP $12.95

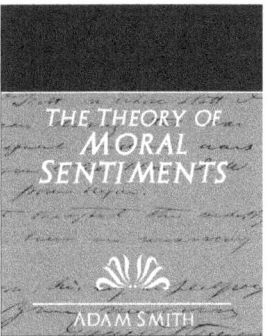

The Theory of Moral Sentiments
Adam Smith

QTY

This work from 1749. contains original theories of conscience amd moral judgment and it is the foundation for systemof morals.

Philosophy   **ISBN:** *1-59462-777-0*   **Pages:536**

MSRP $19.95

Jessica's First Prayer
Hesba Stretton

QTY

In a screened and secluded corner of one of the many railway-bridges which span the streets of London there could be seen a few years ago, from five o'clock every morning until half past eight, a tidily set-out coffee-stall, consisting of a trestle and board, upon which stood two large tin cans, with a small fire of charcoal burning under each so as to keep the coffee boiling during the early hours of the morning when the work-people were thronging into the city on their way to their daily toil...

Pages:84

Childrens   **ISBN:** *1-59462-373-2*   *MSRP $9.95*

My Life and Work
Henry Ford

QTY

Henry Ford revolutionized the world with his implementation of mass production for the Model T automobile. Gain valuable business insight into his life and work with his own auto-biography... "We have only started on our development of our country we have not as yet, with all our talk of wonderful progress, done more than scratch the surface. The progress has been wonderful enough but..."

Pages:300

Biographies/   **ISBN:** *1-59462-198-5*   *MSRP $21.95*

The Art of Cross-Examination
Francis Wellman

QTY

I presume it is the experience of every author, after his first book is published upon an important subject, to be almost overwhelmed with a wealth of ideas and illustrations which could readily have been included in his book, and which to his own mind, at least, seem to make a second edition inevitable. Such certainly was the case with me; and when the first edition had reached its sixth impression in five months, I rejoiced to learn that it seemed to my publishers that the book had met with a sufficiently favorable reception to justify a second and considerably enlarged edition. ...

Reference   **ISBN: *1-59462-647-2***   **Pages:412**   *MSRP $19.95*

On the Duty of Civil Disobedience
Henry David Thoreau

QTY

Thoreau wrote his famous essay, On the Duty of Civil Disobedience, as a protest against an unjust but popular war and the immoral but popular institution of slave-owning. He did more than write—he declined to pay his taxes, and was hauled off to gaol in consequence. Who can say how much this refusal of his hastened the end of the war and of slavery?

Law   **ISBN: *1-59462-747-9***   **Pages:48**   *MSRP $7.45*

Dream Psychology Psychoanalysis for Beginners
Sigmund Freud

QTY

Sigmund Freud, born Sigismund Schlomo Freud (May 6, 1856 - September 23, 1939), was a Jewish-Austrian neurologist and psychiatrist who co-founded the psychoanalytic school of psychology. Freud is best known for his theories of the unconscious mind, especially involving the mechanism of repression; his redefinition of sexual desire as mobile and directed towards a wide variety of objects; and his therapeutic techniques, especially his understanding of transference in the therapeutic relationship and the presumed value of dreams as sources of insight into unconscious desires.

Dream Psychology
Psychoanalysis for Beginners

Sigmund Freud

Psychology   **ISBN: *1-59462-905-6***   **Pages:196**   *MSRP $15.45*

The Miracle of Right Thought
Orison Swett Marden

QTY

Believe with all of your heart that you will do what you were made to do. When the mind has once formed the habit of holding cheerful, happy, prosperous pictures, it will not be easy to form the opposite habit. It does not matter how improbable or how far away this realization may see, or how dark the prospects may be, if we visualize them as best we can, as vividly as possible, hold tenaciously to them and vigorously struggle to attain them, they will gradually become actualized, realized in the life. But a desire, a longing without endeavor, a yearning abandoned or held indifferently will vanish without realization.

Self Help   **ISBN: *1-59462-644-8***   **Pages:360**   *MSRP $25.45*

www.bookjungle.com *email: sales@bookjungle.com fax: 630-214-0564 mail: Book Jungle PO Box 2226 Champaign, IL 61825*

QTY

The Rosicrucian Cosmo-Conception Mystic Christianity *by Max Heindel*   ISBN: *1-59462-188-8*   **$38.95**
The Rosicrucian Cosmo-conception is not dogmatic, neither does it appeal to any other authority than the reason of the student. It is: not controversial, but is: sent forth in the, hope that it may help to clear...   New Age/Religion Pages 646

Abandonment To Divine Providence *by Jean-Pierre de Caussade*   ISBN: *1-59462-228-0*   **$25.95**
"The Rev. Jean Pierre de Caussade was one of the most remarkable spiritual writers of the Society of Jesus in France in the 18th Century. His death took place at Toulouse in 1751. His works have gone through many editions and have been republished...   Inspirational/Religion Pages 400

Mental Chemistry *by Charles Haanel*   ISBN: *1-59462-192-6*   **$23.95**
Mental Chemistry allows the change of material conditions by combining and appropriately utilizing the power of the mind. Much like applied chemistry creates something new and unique out of careful combinations of chemicals the mastery of mental chemistry...   New Age Pages 354

The Letters of Robert Browning and Elizabeth Barret Barrett 1845-1846 vol II   ISBN: *1-59462-193-4*   **$35.95**
by Robert Browning and Elizabeth Barrett   Biographies Pages 596

Gleanings In Genesis (volume I) *by Arthur W. Pink*   ISBN: *1-59462-130-6*   **$27.45**
Appropriately has Genesis been termed "the seed plot of the Bible" for in it we have, in germ form, almost all of the great doctrines which are afterwards fully developed in the books of Scripture which follow...   Religion/Inspirational Pages 420

The Master Key *by L. W. de Laurence*   ISBN: *1-59462-001-6*   **$30.95**
In no branch of human knowledge has there been a more lively increase of the spirit of research during the past few years than in the study of Psychology, Concentration and Mental Discipline. The requests for authentic lessons in Thought Control, Mental Discipline and...   New Age/Business Pages 422

The Lesser Key Of Solomon Goetia *by L. W. de Laurence*   ISBN: *1-59462-092-X*   **$9.95**
This translation of the first book of the "Lernegton" which is now for the first time made accessible to students of Talismanic Magic was done, after careful collation and edition, from numerous Ancient Manuscripts in Hebrew, Latin, and French...   New Age/Occult Pages 92

Rubaiyat Of Omar Khayyam *by Edward Fitzgerald*   ISBN: *1-59462-332-5*   **$13.95**
Edward Fitzgerald, whom the world has already learned, in spite of his own efforts to remain within the shadow of anonymity, to look upon as one of the rarest poets of the century, was born at Bredfield, in Suffolk, on the 31st of March, 1809. He was the third son of John Purcell...   Music Pages 172

Ancient Law *by Henry Maine*   ISBN: *1-59462-128-4*   **$29.95**
The chief object of the following pages is to indicate some of the earliest ideas of mankind, as they are reflected in Ancient Law, and to point out the relation of those ideas to modern thought.   Religion/History Pages 452

Far-Away Stories *by William J. Locke*   ISBN: *1-59462-129-2*   **$19.45**
"Good wine needs no bush, but a collection of mixed vintages does. And this book is just such a collection. Some of the stories I do not want to remain buried for ever in the museum files of dead magazine-numbers an author's not unpardonable vanity..."   Fiction Pages 272

Life of David Crockett *by David Crockett*   ISBN: *1-59462-250-7*   **$27.45**
"Colonel David Crockett was one of the most remarkable men of the times in which he lived. Born in humble life, but gifted with a strong will, an indomitable courage, and unremitting perseverance...   Biographies/New Age Pages 424

Lip-Reading *by Edward Nitchie*   ISBN: *1-59462-206-X*   **$25.95**
Edward B. Nitchie, founder of the New York School for the Hard of Hearing, now the Nitchie School of Lip-Reading, Inc, wrote "LIP-READING Principles and Practice". The development and perfecting of this meritorious work on lip-reading was an undertaking...   How-to Pages 400

A Handbook of Suggestive Therapeutics, Applied Hypnotism, Psychic Science   ISBN: *1-59462-214-0*   **$24.95**
by Henry Munro   Health/New Age/Health/Self-help Pages 376

A Doll's House: and Two Other Plays *by Henrik Ibsen*   ISBN: *1-59462-112-8*   **$19.95**
Henrik Ibsen created this classic when in revolutionary 1848 Rome. Introducing some striking concepts in playwriting for the realist genre, this play has been studied the world over.   Fiction/Classics/Plays 308

The Light of Asia *by sir Edwin Arnold*   ISBN: *1-59462-204-3*   **$13.95**
In this poetic masterpiece, Edwin Arnold describes the life and teachings of Buddha. The man who was to become known as Buddha to the world was born as Prince Gautama of India but he rejected the worldly riches and abandoned the reigns of power when...   Religion/History/Biographies Pages 170

The Complete Works of Guy de Maupassant *by Guy de Maupassant*   ISBN: *1-59462-157-8*   **$16.95**
"For days and days, nights and nights, I had dreamed of that first kiss which was to consecrate our engagement, and I knew not on what spot I should put my lips..."   Fiction/Classics Pages 240

The Art of Cross-Examination *by Francis L. Wellman*   ISBN: *1-59462-309-0*   **$26.95**
Written by a renowned trial lawyer, Wellman imparts his experience and uses case studies to explain how to use psychology to extract desired information through questioning.   How-to/Science/Reference Pages 408

Answered or Unanswered? *by Louisa Vaughan*   ISBN: *1-59462-248-5*   **$10.95**
Miracles of Faith in China   Religion Pages 112

The Edinburgh Lectures on Mental Science (1909) *by Thomas*   ISBN: *1-59462-008-3*   **$11.95**
This book contains the substance of a course of lectures recently given by the writer in the Queen Street Hail, Edinburgh. Its purpose is to indicate the Natural Principles governing the relation between Mental Action and Material Conditions...   New Age/Psychology Pages 148

Ayesha *by H. Rider Haggard*   ISBN: *1-59462-301-5*   **$24.95**
Verily and indeed it is the unexpected that happens! Probably if there was one person upon the earth from whom the Editor of this, and of a certain previous history, did not expect to hear again...   Classics Pages 380

Ayala's Angel *by Anthony Trollope*   ISBN: *1-59462-352-X*   **$29.95**
The two girls were both pretty, but Lucy who was twenty-one who supposed to be simple and comparatively unattractive, whereas Ayala was credited, as her Bombwhat romantic name might show, with poetic charm and a taste for romance. Ayala when her father died was nineteen...   Fiction Pages 484

The American Commonwealth *by James Bryce*   ISBN: *1-59462-286-8*   **$34.45**
An interpretation of American democratic political theory. It examines political mechanics and society from the perspective of Scotsman James Bryce   Politics Pages 572

Stories of the Pilgrims *by Margaret P. Pumphrey*   ISBN: *1-59462-116-0*   **$17.95**
This book explores pilgrims religious oppression in England as well as their escape to Holland and eventual crossing to America on the Mayflower, and their early days in New England...   History Pages 268

QTY

The Fasting Cure by *Sinclair Upton*   ISBN: *1-59462-222-1* **$13.95**
In the Cosmopolitan Magazine for May, 1910, and in the Contemporary Review (London) for April, 1910, I published an article dealing with my experiences in fasting. I have written a great many magazine articles, but never one which attracted so much attention... New Age/Self Help/Health Pages 164

Hebrew Astrology by *Sepharial*   ISBN: *1-59462-308-2* **$13.45**
In these days of advanced thinking it is a matter of common observation that we have left many of the old landmarks behind and that we are now pressing forward to greater heights and to a wider horizon than that which represented the mind-content of our progenitors... Astrology Pages 144

Thought Vibration or The Law of Attraction in the Thought World   ISBN: *1-59462-127-6* **$12.95**

by *William Walker Atkinson*   *Psychology/Religion Pages 144*

Optimism by *Helen Keller*   ISBN: *1-59462-108-X* **$15.95**
Helen Keller was blind, deaf, and mute since 19 months old, yet famously learned how to overcome these handicaps, communicate with the world, and spread her lectures promoting optimism. An inspiring read for everyone... Biographies/Inspirational Pages 84

Sara Crewe by *Frances Burnett*   ISBN: *1-59462-360-0* **$9.45**
In the first place, Miss Minchin lived in London. Her home was a large, dull, tall one, in a large, dull square, where all the houses were alike, and all the sparrows were alike, and where all the door-knockers made the same heavy sound... Childrens/Classic Pages 88

The Autobiography of Benjamin Franklin by *Benjamin Franklin*   ISBN: *1-59462-135-7* **$24.95**
The Autobiography of Benjamin Franklin has probably been more extensively read than any other American historical work, and no other book of its kind has had such ups and downs of fortune. Franklin lived for many years in England, where he was agent... Biographies/History Pages 332

Name	
Email	
Telephone	
Address	
City, State ZIP	

☐ **Credit Card**   ☐ **Check / Money Order**

Credit Card Number	
Expiration Date	
Signature	

Please Mail to: Book Jungle
PO Box 2226
Champaign, IL 61825
or Fax to: 630-214-0564

ORDERING INFORMATION

web: *www.bookjungle.com*
email: *sales@bookjungle.com*
fax: *630-214-0564*
mail: *Book Jungle PO Box 2226 Champaign, IL 61825*
or PayPal *to sales@bookjungle.com*

Please contact us for bulk discounts

DIRECT-ORDER TERMS

**20% Discount if You Order
Two or More Books**
Free Domestic Shipping!
Accepted: Master Card, Visa,
Discover, American Express